MW00638610

3

The Rabbit
Who Didn't
Like
Carrots

P.F. Armstrong

Copyright © 2023 by P. F. Armstrong.
All rights reserved. No part of this publication may be
reproduced, distributed, or transmitted in any form or by
any means, including photocopying, recording, or other
electronic or mechanical methods, without the prior written
permission of the publisher, except in the case of brief
quotations embodied in critical reviews and certain other
noncommercial uses permitted by copyright law.

For permission requests, write to the publisher,
at the address below.

Artwork by: Beth Rose West

Edited by: Innovative Editing, LLC Lancaster, PA

P. F. Armstrong
Lancaster, Pennsylvania, 17603
The Rabbit Who Didn't Like Carrots/P. F. Armstrong. —1st
ed.
ISBN: 978-1-7341962-2-1

P.F. Armstrong
1740 Wilderness Road
Lancaster, PA. 17603

Dedicated to those whose courageous tenacity to truth
brought this story to life,
with special appreciation to
Nicholas, Claire and Eleanor.

Table of Contents

Then God said: Let the earth bring forth every kind of living creature: tame animals, crawling things, and every kind of wild animal. And so it happened: God made every kind of wild animal, every kind of tame animal, and every kind of thing that crawls on the ground. God saw that it was good.

From Genesis, NABRE translation

Be who you are, and be that well.

Francis DeSales

Prologue

As parents, we take on a sacred duty. To live up to that duty requires us to understand the foundations of truth, of beauty, of goodness. Thankfully, we do not need to discover them - they have been revealed to us. The wonder of life reveals them. The Laws of Mother Nature are anchored in them.

Our children have a naturally inclined trust in our parenting. When we fail as parents to live up to our sacred duty we violate that trust and compromise our children. Tragically, we don't just fail them. We fail to ensure the well-being of future generations.

When we look at the diversity of life, we see a remarkable concert orchestrated by Mother Nature. We know all too well what discord happens when we, as humans, try to interfere with that concert.

I have created many stories for my grandchildren. Frequently we start with situations that sound implausible, and the story flows from there. Thus, this tale was born.

The rabbit who didn't like carrots was so intriguing a theme that my now teenage cousin asked for five years when I'd write this story. Neither of us really knew any plot for this vegetable of an idea.

But then a plot formed with a calling to share the story. The carrot conundrum helped me wonder: What would the story be if animals had the free will to abandon the sources of truth, beauty and goodness?

1

A Snuggly World

---

*"The rabbit family, like all animals,
knew that every day was spent
searching for food, and not being
food."*

Romi slowly opened her sleepy eyes.   From the narrowest of peeks, she could see the gray light of a cloudy morning. Subtle rays illuminated the inside of the burrow.

Romi didn't want to move. She was more than content to continue snuggling, staying warm alongside her brothers: Risky, Rowdy, Ruffy, and Rambi, as well as her sisters: Rumbly and Reya. As the seven bunnies began to squirm into wakefulness, they worked to pack themselves together all the more tightly.

There was a hint of frost on the ground, typical for the early spring. With the sun struggling to make an appearance from behind the thick clouds, the morning remained chilly. Because the cold could kill them, the bunnies knew to pack themselves tightly together. Doing that, along with their soft and warm fur coats, protected them from the harsh weather outside.

Romi looked out the burrow hole. Her mother, Rajina, like all rabbit mothers, knew that the cold was not the biggest threat. She had spent the night guarding the entrance. The litter's father, Rater, was nearby doing likewise. Both were alert to protect their family from a danger that would not be overcome by the sun. It was where this family of rabbits stood in the predator-prey world.

The rabbit family, like all animals, knew that every day was spent searching for food and not being food. They were a favorite meal of many animals. The dark nights were full of nocturnal predators, like the foxes, weasels and even those silly house cats.

Romi knew that despite how much she'd rather continue to live as a bunny, snuggled warmly in her parent's care, that one day she'd need to be the one who did the protecting. Like her parents were doing for her now, she'd be the one to help little ones sharpen and summon their keen rabbit senses to be ever alert to impending predator danger.

Ruffy, Rowdy and Rambi started to stir. These three were the big boys of the litter and they usually got their way. Romi was the runt. Born last, born small, she was always struggling to get enough milk. She did not think this was fair, nor had she asked to be the runt of the litter. But even when she pretended to be big and tough, the fact remained. Romi was the runt, the weakest and smallest member of Rajina's early spring litter.

Romi's father, Rater, had been consistently and patiently instructing Romi that being a runt was just a fact of life for her. She could not wish it away. Rater pointed out that while the whole litter had the essence, as he did, of being rabbits, Romi also had the essence of being a runt rabbit. He taught her the truth. Runts have a tough time in life.

Romi believed her father, even though she didn't want to. Sometimes she would act all big and tough in their rabbit play, but every time, either Ruffy, Rowdy or Rambi would put her in her place. Rumbly and Reya, though also larger than Romi, would be similarly crowded out, in all the shoving, trying to get to their mother's milk.

Romi's brother, Risky, was the one that Mother had to look out for the most. For unexplained reasons, he was the one who was always at the edge of the burrow, looking out. Mother often had to pull him back in. An alert hawk could easily snatch such a small snack from the burrow's edge. Risky would grumble that his mother would not let him be the indestructible super bunny he thought he was. She would remind him that he was a bunny, regardless of what his emotions or imagination wanted him to believe.

But it wasn't really Mother or Father Rabbit who provided all the rules.

Like all animals since the beginning of time, the rabbit family strove to respect the laws of that other Mother, namely, Mother Nature. Rajina and Rater respected this well. They were constantly guiding, training and

5

disciplining their litter to respect her laws. They frequently explained that everything was put in place by the Master Craftsman, and that they were put in place in a certain order, an order that ensured that our world would sustain life. They explained that Mother Nature was sort of like the guardian of that plan. That like a Craftsman creates a craft, there are those who then care for that craft with a loving discipline and caring diligence. Mother Nature protected the rhythm that the Master Craftsman intended so that the craft would reflect his craftsmanship. This craft was like a composed song, and Mother Nature made sure that the notes and rhythm intended by the Composer were played properly. Mother Nature's laws were nothing more than a way for each living creature, each physical entity, to be in symphony with the underlying beauty of the Master Craftsman's composition.

This rhythm of life, orchestrated by Mother Nature, did feel unfair to runts, especially runts who were the prey of so many predators.

2

Essence to Exist

"The Craftsman gave each of us our essence."

Morning breakfast, courtesy of the milk that the Master Craftsman gave Mother Rabbit, was delicious as always. But today's breakfast would be the last one that Rajina would provide directly for her litter. Today was the day they'd leave the burrow. Today's breakfast was to give them the energy to be alert and ready to learn.

Rater used this special day to share with his bunnies the realities of life. He had them snuggle comfortably in the back of the burrow. The sun shone behind him as he blocked the entrance, just in case an unwanted predator decided to make them a meal. Rater looked at each of them, one at a time.

He then began to speak softly.

"The Craftsman gave each of us our essence. Actually, he gave all living creatures their essence. Now, that's kind of a funny word, so let me put it this way. The essence is sort of like the essentials, so to speak, that we have been provided by the Craftsman. With that essence, along with the rhythm set by Mother Nature, we have the best chances of survival, and ability to find a mate and go forth and multiply. You see, it's a fact: we are prey. And that seems unfair to us, but we have other advantages. One of them is our ability to have a lot of bunnies. That is how we make sure that there will always be rabbits in the world."

"And guess what? It's worked! But it only works when all of us pay attention to, understand, respect, nurture and use our essence as rabbits, our 'rabbitness'. That then helps us to exist as rabbits are supposed to exist.
He eyes brightened. "Tomorrow will start that existence for you in a new way."

The bunnies' ears were completely erect as their father pointed towards the burrow opening, continuing his lesson. "You will be out of the burrow. You will nibble on new foods.

He narrowed his eyes and lowered his voice to nearly a whisper. "And you will be the primary target of every nearby predator."

He stood up straight and resumed a voice of authority "But, if you pay attention to your essence, your rabbitness, you will have the best chance to exist as a rabbit."

The bunnies were still too young, too inexperienced to fully appreciate the wisdom they had just heard. Of course, why would they not want to use their rabbitness? In some ways, Father's talk was as obvious as it was hard to appreciate. Sometimes good wisdom is like that.

The rabbit patriarch continued, "Think of it this way. The Master Craftsman has made the colors and the sounds. The essence of blue is its blueness. Blue can't pretend or try to be red. The essence of a screech is its screechiness. It can't pretend or try to be the sound of a waterfall. Mother Nature then uses these colors and sounds to teach us how to understand and live in the world. If a wounded animal wanted to use a sound like a waterfall instead of a screech, we'd never know the difference between being in danger or not. So, the essence gives each piece of this world a way and a place to exist. It is the same with your rabbit essence."

Father paused, and then added, "So, what do you think are some of the gifts that you have as rabbits that give you your essence, your rabbitness?"

Romi was surprised that this was now what sounded like a test. Unbeknownst to her, their wise father was already preparing their minds to think on their own, to be ready to face the outside world.

Reya spoke up first. "We have great fur that keeps us warm!"

Rater nodded his agreement. "Way to get us started, Reya."

Rowdy already sensed that this was now a game. "We have eyes that can see all around and up and down!"

Rambi quickly added, "We have really powerful hind legs…or, at least I hope I do!"

Rater smiled, while the rest of the bunnies giggled. "Don't worry, Rambi, I'm sure you do."

Romi started to worry. She was a runt. Her legs weren't as strong as the others. That was proven just in her inability to force her way past her siblings for nursing. Was she not quite a rabbit?

Ruffy scratched his ear, and as if that was the prompt he needed, spoke up. "Our ears!"

"Anything else?" prompted their father.

The bunnies sort of stared at him hoping that he'd just give them the next answer.

Rater smiled. "Believe it or not, even our little tail!"

The bunnies were puzzled. They had seen other animals - the squirrel family, the fox, the groundhog, the mice, and even the birds. They all had really cool tails. But bunnies only had this little white piece of fluff.

Reya voiced her puzzlement. "Wait a minute, dear father. It's almost like we didn't even get a tail. How could that be a gift?"

Father had been expecting such a question. "You see, sometimes what we don't have is also a gift. And when we are making a dash into a burrow, we don't have to worry about a predator grabbing our tail. And, we don't really need it for balance like birds and squirrels… so that is part of our rabbit essence."

Rater then peered out of the burrow. He turned back to his bunnies who were soon to be rabbits. "I will not remind you of what all is out in that yard when you leave the burrow tomorrow."

The rabbit family lived in a yard that was frequented by humans, farmers by trade. Rajina and Rater had chosen this location, as their keen noses sensed that the yard had never been fouled by strange chemicals that other humans seemed to have on their greens.

The rabbits never quite understood humans, yet they did not let that lack of understanding keep them from appreciating that those human gardens provided a handy buffet. Rajina and Rater had made their burrow so that it was tightly hidden in a tuft of grass at the edge of the raised bed garden. They had learned that the corner of its wooden sides provided a perfect hiding place and saved them a bit of digging too.

The space between the boxes was never bothered by that noisy grass chopping machine, which was a menace to unsuspecting rabbits. That meant that this clump of orchard grass, at the corner of the box, was rarely cut. On the inside corner of the box was a clump of chives. While these were not a rabbit's sought-after food, the chives made for a protective barrier to the small hole they had made in the corner of the box.

Their home was not invisible, and the scent of their safe shelter provided a clue to curious predators. Even that clumsy, goofy chocolate lab, that was always with the humans, had found their burrow. But the location was just too inconvenient for him to dig a hole large enough for that very large snout of his.

When Romi peered out of the burrow, she could see the big azalea bush near one of the buildings. She had been told that their neighbor rabbits lived there.

Rajina entered the burrow as Rater made his way out, looking carefully in all directions. As they exchanged places, a dash of sunshine burst into the burrow. The bunnies were excited to learn what sunlight felt like.

Rajina looked her progeny in the eyes, one by one. She spoke with a serious but caring tone. "You see, once you leave this burrow, you are just one of many creatures out there. They are all tucked into their own homes - some in the ground, some in the trees, some in the bushes. For example, as you may have seen from our burrow, the squirrel family lives in that massive maple tree there."

Romi nodded in agreement. She had seen squirrels going in and out of the big hole in the main trunk of the tree.

"Now, we have friendly agreements with most of our fellow creatures. The squirrels are rodents and they spend most of their time gathering nuts and seeds. We don't have the stomach or teeth for that. Remember, they are rodents, and we are not." Rajina had a bit of rabbit pride in her voice while saying that last sentence.

"We don't eat what they eat, so we have no reason to quarrel. And, squirrels have the same predators as us, so when they send out a warning, we should take heed. The groundhog is harmless, though he does eat the same greens we do. Actually, he can eat quite a bit. He's a bit grumpy and may be eating all of our favorite foods by midsummer. Pokey possum doesn't bother anybody, and he eats all those ticks, so he is a good friend to have around."

Rajina's voice took on a deeper, darker tone. "But those are our friendly neighbors. Remember we are prey. While you may not see them as frequently, predators are always there. We are one of their favorite victims. The fox family lives down in the wooded area. While father and I have watched over the burrow, we have seen them lurking around quite a bit. There is also a crazy fisher cat out there. Thankfully, there's only one and he normally stays in the woods. And then, in the air, we have hawks and owls. They are the worst. Quiet. Fast. Deadly. So, we need to watch around and up. The squirrels are especially helpful keeping us alert to those killers."

The bunnies, who moments ago were thinking themselves ready for the outside world, armed with their rabbit essence, were now not quite so sure.

Reya, whose mind was now very troubled, mumbled, "But Mother dear, if it's that dangerous, can't we just stay here? Can't we go to a place where there are no foxes, or owls, or hawks? And why do they have to pick on us?"

Rajina knew the question was on their minds, even before Reya had voiced it.

"My dear bunnies, I wish that I could let you loose in a carefree, green world. Where all you had to do was eat, meet a mate, and have bunnies of your own. But that is not our world. And we may not always understand the why. But we are here today because all rabbits... my parents, my parents' parents, their parents... going all the way back to what might have been the first rabbits... used their rabbit essence, and, despite the army of predators, we are here today. So the real answer is to live your essence so that you can live your existence, and that existence will allow future generations of rabbits to exist."

Romi could see how much their mother truly cared for them. She could see that the one who gave her birth would truly love to send them unburdened in a carefree world, where they had no worries.

However, Romi had a burning question she just had to ask. "But Mother dear, I'm just a runt. So, I don't have all the rabbit gifts. I don't want to be a runty rabbit."

Rajina looked at her smallest litter member. A pain pierced her heart. She knew that runts never had the same chances to escape the dangers of the predator world. But she also knew that she could not mislead her litter runt and pretend that runtiness was something the bunny could wish away.

"My little Romi, you are right... in a way. Being a runt means that you need to rely even more on the rabbit essences you do have. You may not be as big, or as fast, but you still have hearing. You have a small size that maybe fits where bigger rabbits or prey can't. But, don't ever think that makes you less of a rabbit... it just makes you a slower, smaller rabbit."

3
Existential Essence

> *"Life is short and you need to make
> the most of it."*

In a burrow nearby, the young mother rabbit Rebil brought more soft grass into her burrow. She wanted to do everything perfect, fastidious about every detail. She was constantly learning from her good friend and neighbor, Rajina. Rebil and her mate Redneg were first time parents. Both of them had tremendous respect for Rajina and Rater, who had pointed out how to live well on this human farm. The rookie parents were glad to have such confident and caring rabbits as mentors.

Rebil hollered over towards Rajina's burrow. "Are you still ready to have them all head out tomorrow?"

She heard a quick "yup", and assumed that Rajina was still nursing. Rajina had shared with Rebil when she and Rater would let their bunnies first go out. Rebil found it easy to get Redneg's immediate agreement to let their own litter out on that same day.

Redneg liked the idea that all the bunnies would venture out together at the same time. He thought there would be some safety in numbers. Besides, Rebil and Redneg thought they could do better than their mentors and the first day out would be a chance to demonstrate that maybe they had a better way of parenting.

Rebil and Redneg looked at their five offspring. The little girls, Rial and Rispy, and the three boys, Raspy, Rompy and Roomy. Roomy was the largest of the litter and they had no worries about him. They did not really have a runt of the litter, and for that they were thankful.

As all rabbit parents, they were extremely proud of their progeny. And since this was their first litter, they were determined to be the kindest parents ever.

Since tomorrow was going to be the first day out, the parents knew that they needed to prepare the group for life outside the burrow, and their journey to rabbit-hood.

Rebil looked at her litter. She started speaking with a tone that she hoped would instill a careful confidence. "My dear little ones. Tomorrow will be your first day outside. You will get to meet our rabbit friends, and you will be able to play with their litter. They too will be having their first day out of the burrow. Your job is to explore, to find out what you like and don't like. There are more than enough greens to eat out there, and even a few tasty pods. You will need to be on the watch for predators, and your father and I, along with Rater and Rajina, will be keeping a close eye. We will be sounding

16

the alarm to get to safety whenever we see a hint of trouble. So, pay close attention to us."

Rial spoke up, "I'm not sure I want to leave our burrow, Mother. I've heard the sounds at night, and it seems scary out there."

Rompy joined in, "Yes, Mother. I'm awake at night and I hear them also."

Rebil's heart ached as the two voiced their fears.

"I think you'll feel better once you feel the freedom you have out there."

Rispy was straining to see out the burrow past her mother. "I can't wait to run around that grassy yard. It looks like there are hundreds of things for us to eat out there."

Raspy joined in with his sister's excitement. "Me too. I can smell some things that seem like they will be delicious."

Roomy did not look outside but kept his eyes on his mother, seeing if she was going to allow them to nurse some more. The largest of the litter, he was always ready for another meal.

Redneg poked his head into the burrow. "Are you guys excited about tomorrow?"

Rebil realized that father rabbit wanted to share some words with their young charges as well. They exchanged places, and Rebil made a thorough scan of the area near the burrow.

Redneg began, "You know that tomorrow you start defining who you'll want to be. You get to decide how you want to exist in the world. Each day opens up new experiences. You can figure out what experiences you like and what you don't like."

Their father made gestures towards the opening of the burrow, and his voice took on more of an air of authority as he continued his teaching. "Now, you'll be playing with other rabbits. Some of them may try to tell you how to be or what to like. You don't need to listen to them. Don't feel bound by what other rabbits are doing or tell you. You get to make your existence what you want it to be. The world is a wonderful, exciting place, full of possibilities, but life is short and you need to make the most of it. You know your mother and I will respect however you want to live. Just be who you think you were meant to be. There will be lots of animals out there. Some will be bigger than us, some smaller. But you get to figure out how you want to be and how you want to fit in."

Rompy wiggled with excitement at the thought that he could be whatever he wanted. Even though he had no idea what that freedom really meant or what burdens it would actually bear, he thought it sounded excitingly open.

Rispy whispered to Rompy, "I don't really understand. We haven't even been out of our burrow yet. I'm not sure I even know what all the animals will look like to tell them apart."

Raspy, the big eater of the litter, spoke up, "I am looking forward to eating as many green things as I can find."

Redneg heard Raspy's excited anticipation. "Well Raspy... and I say this for all of you, don't think that you only eat green things. Actually, the humans will throw out some items that are also delicious, like the tops of carrots and sometimes apples. You'll see when we get out there."

Rial had been absorbed in the idea of getting to decide for herself. "Father dear, how will we know that what we want will be good for us or even make sense? I'd like to be the biggest one in the litter so that I can always get Mother's milk, but I can't."

Redneg was touched by his daughter's keen attention to what he had said. But now that she stated it back, he had to think about the statement himself. It had flowed out so naturally even though what he had said stood at odds with what Mother Nature guided and the Master Craftsman instilled in all creatures.

Redneg recalled how he first heard that sentiment. It was something that creatures started calling the "new thinking." It had appealed to Redneg in a way that fed his pride. It had appealed to him as something he wanted to begin to pass down to his children.

One of tenets of the new thinking that especially stroked his ego was the calling to each creature to assert their own will. He did not really understand the depth of what that meant, but his superficial attraction to the idea was enough.

Patting Rial gently on the head, he concluded, "Don't worry. You will be getting better at asserting your will. If you will it, you can do it."

P. F. Armstrong

4
Gabbadon

---

*"To make the deception all the more
delicious, the message had to be
cloaked in what appeared to be good,
appeared to be true, appeared to be
beauty."*

G abbadon smacked his lips. He savored the unlucky fly
he had stealthily snagged with his lightning-fast jaws.
He glanced around to see if any other unsuspecting
insects were nearby.

Gabbadon was enjoying the cloudy day which made his
camouflaging all the more undetectable. He did not like
the light. His work was best done in the gray darkness of
an overcast day.

The guileful gecko was feeling quite smug. While he
believed IN the Craftsman, he did not BELIEVE the

Craftsman. Gabbadon had long ago decided that the Master Craftsman was not the loving maker of all living things. He could only view the Craftsman as a competitor, a tyrant who demanded the attention of each creature.

Gabbadon's eyes scanned to and fro, his body not making a single motion. A small beetle was gnawing on a piece of decaying wood. As the gecko waited for his next snack to work itself closer, he fed his pride. He was Gabbadon, and he was way too important to be bound by the rules of Mother Nature. In his self-centered absorption, he could only see her guidance as a nuisance and refused to have faith in the goodness of her ways. He only wanted to follow his own ways, to be his own boss and to make his own rules.

In pulling away from the truth of the Craftsman, Gabbadon entered into a world of constant thirst. This was not a physical thirst, but a thirst for meaning, a thirst for power, a thirst for belonging. He could not be content with his own personal hate of the Craftsman. He wanted others to join him in his rejection of the Master.

But Gabbadon wanted something more than that. He wanted all animals to follow his rules, to follow in his footsteps of rebellion against the Master Craftsman and Mother Nature. He knew to do that he had to get them to mistrust the Craftsman and the Mother. And when they let go of that trust, then he'd be able to fill their emptiness with his own dark scheme.

The beetle inched closer.

He had persuaded many animals to join him in his rejection of the good and the beauty of what the Master put in place. He found that he enjoyed when they joined him in his dark world. It usually led to their untimely demise as they stepped outside the laws of Mother Nature. Their leaving this world was of no concern to Gabbadon. Actually, quite the opposite, as their decaying corpses attracted flies and harbored maggots. Gabbadon loved flies and maggots.

Today, he was feeling rather smug. Gabbadon had found a way to pull many animals away from their respect of the Master, to defy the loving rules of the Mother. He firmly believed that misery loves company.

Gabbadon realized that it was easier to convince animals that there was no Master Craftsman than to persuade them to turn their backs on the Craftsman. The reason was obvious, as deciding to not believe was a lazier way to distance oneself from the Master than outright rebellion. Gabbadon could rely on that mental sloth to be his ally. Gabbadon knew that when he obscured their ability to see the goodness of truth, he could sneak past their conscience and into their minds.

He loved this new tactic, as it came with a delightfully devious side effect. If animals dropped their belief in the source of truth, good and beauty, then they'd become blind to their opposites of deception, evil and misery. Letting go of the Master Craftsman would allow them to let go of ultimate truth.

His smugness was because he now had a few animals who would serve his purpose. The help came in the form of a trio of fellow amphibians. They were a new breed of animal in terms of their willingness to question all that the animal kingdom had relied on to successfully inhabit the planet for millennia. They had a way of explaining

23

their ideas that had a seductive appeal, perfectly camouflaging the underlying deception. It was an approach that the gecko could genuinely appreciate.

The beetle wandered towards another piece of rotted wood. The gecko smiled to himself. With a lightning fast movement, the wood loving bug was now his snack.

Gabbadon realized that the time was ripe. He had influenced enough animals into considering the words of these three supposedly intellectual amphibians as being a refreshing 'new thinking'.

And Gabbadon took it one step further. He convinced the followers of the new thinking to consider anyone still respecting the 'old thinking' about a Craftsman and the Mother to be painted as being bigoted, as unwilling to open their minds to new truths. Divisiveness was Gabbadon's ally.

To make the deception all the more delicious, the message had to be cloaked in what appeared to be good, appeared to be true, appeared to be beauty. After all, isn't that what is at the core of any good deception? To sandwich a lie between two truths?

The words of these three would play on each animal's ego and pride in the present moment. Once the words wedged doubt in their minds, that would be the crack in trust the gecko and his henchmen were waiting for. That crack would serve as the gateway to what the gecko truly wanted. To cast off the Master Craftsman and declare oneself as one's own craftsman.

Gabbadon knew that while they would seem free of one Master, they would unknowingly be inviting in another master. And he fully knew how to be that deceptively invited master.

His smugness turned him a new shade of dark gray. Soon he would prove to the Master Craftsman that he, Gabbadon the gecko, was the rightful master of his fellow creation's minds and bodies.

A fly landed on a remnant of decaying crayfish. As it worked intently on tearing some food from the skeletal membrane, it took no notice of the gray lump on a nearby rock. Gabbadon kept himself perfectly still. He would prove yet again that he was indeed the lord of flies.

P. F. Armstrong

5
Minds Over Matter

> *"We need to ply their minds with the idea that a principle we'll call 'freedom' is the core value of existence."*

The salamander skittered onto the moss covered rock. The spray from the small waterfall kept it moist, making a most delightful place for the little amphibian. Sarty considered himself a very clever salamander. His contrarian ideas were served by his smooth yet intellectual delivery, and had established for him a sizable number of followers. He thought that his popularity was evidential proof that his ideas were truth. Sarty's ego fed on that popularity, emboldening him in his conviction of his own views.

Sarty snagged a slow flying gnat, enjoying a quick snack while he waited for the others.

Hopping up from a small pool, just downstream of the waterfall, Fucho made his presence known quickly. The intellectually snobby frog had many similar ideas to the salamander. Fucho was fussy about his name being pronounced properly, insisting that he was fu-CHO, not FU-cho.

Climbing down from her hiding place on the red twig dogwood, Nishy came within speaking distance of the other two. She nodded a silent greeting, slithering her trim newt body onto a mossy rock. The intense newt thought of herself as the author of each idea that the salamander and frog now expounded and expanded upon.

The three of them together had been steadily building a very different and oddly convincing view of the world. What they were each espousing stood in stark contrast to the beliefs and values that had been held since time began. What was noticeably different in their new thinking was how they discarded any need to see the good, the beautiful and the transcendent as endearing or even necessary attributes for life. Their preaching seemed to disregard each creature's part in the orchestra of life. Instead, they dwelled on how each creature saw its own existence.

Interestingly, there was an almost paradoxical twist in their thinking. In convincing creatures to abandon the long held truth to live to one obvious essence, they were offering the fleeting moment of one's existence as the lifeline to the meaning of one's life. But in reality, they knew that was not a lifeline at all, giving them reason to consider life as somewhat absurd, almost to the point of meaningless.

But this was how they hooked creatures into the mire of their confusion. They had a recommended escape from this dire senseless existence. That escape was based on elevating the pursuit of personal freedom as the highest good.

Their logic cast the Master Craftsman and Mother Nature into being seen as freedom robbing slave owners, not caretakers. By transferring the core of truth from the creator to the creature, they opened the door to everyone having their own truth. For the new thinkers, this was the gateway to true personal freedom.

Gazing from a distance, but still hidden from their view, was Gabbadon. He could hardly keep his glee from bursting out. How he had worked the minds of these three so that they would spread a belief that betrayed all notions of a Master Craftsman and Mother Nature. He did not care that their departure from knowing the Craftsman had become a total disbelief in the very presence of the Master. Gabbadon knew all too well that the Master Craftsman existed but hated that the Craftsman sought his obedience. However, with these three, the crafty gecko could start to build a growing coalition of animals who denied the Craftsman's existence.

Sarty began to speak, "My fellow new thinkers, it's time for us to build a broader awareness of our new ideas. If we are only believed by a few, we will always be seen as a passing fad, a whiff of an idea that never took root. I don't know about you two, but in a life that's so short, only one's ideas have any lasting value. We need to pull more animals away from the stale idea of what they call Mother Nature. We need to pull more animals away from the notion that the Master Craftsman has imbued all life

P. F. Armstrong

with an underlying natural science. We need to ply their minds with the idea that a principle we'll call 'freedom' is the core value of existence."

From her soft spot on the moss, Nishy piped in, "That is a very good foundation. It will allow us to convince them that there are no pre-ordained paths assigned to us by a Master Craftsman or by Mother Nature. That each animal has ultimate freedom when they can decide what they are, not based on their essence from some Master Craftsman or the supposed laws of Mother Nature."

The frog had been nodding agreeably to what the salamander and newt were saying. He positioned himself a bit more comfortably on his rock, almost invisible amongst the patches of algae. His distinctive voice began. "We must enlighten the animals to see that this myth of obeying Mother Nature is nothing more than a pervasive and perverse plot to keep them under the yoke of the prevailing power structure."

Gabbadon felt a surge of vile excitement at these words. Hearing his cold-blooded agents of confusion explain how to cast aside the Master Craftsman caused him to change from his camouflage brown to a dull black, silhouetting him against his log.

6
The World Matters

> *"...they knew how critical it would be
> for them to continue to nurture each
> young rabbit's gifts so that they could
> survive in Mother Nature's drama."*

As with each morning since they had been born, Rajina nursed her litter after being on watch all night. They hungrily suckled the nectar that she bore. Rajina gave a silent thanks to the Master Craftsman who provided this gift, the essence of her maternal female nature. She was quietly grateful for Mother's guidance to follow her maternal instincts so that her litter would survive. Rajina knew that without the essence of being a female rabbit and without the rhythm of Mother Nature, there would be no future generations of rabbits.

Rajina realized that today's nursing needed to provide something more, as this would be their first day out of the burrow. She felt both a stab of fear and a sense of relief that this was their last nursing. Her fear was the cold reality that her young ones had to quickly put into practice what she and Rater were about to show them. The rabbit parents would be instructing their young on some of the great, and not so great, edibles that were just beginning to poke their heads up from the slowly thawing earth.

As they finished nursing, the bunnies started bouncing with energized excitement.

Risky was already at the burrow opening. "Let's get going! It looks fantastic out there!"

Rajina smiled at the unbridled exuberance of her most adventurous offspring. "Ok, ok... wait for me to lead you out. Your father should be nearby. Can you see him?"

Risky poked his head out of the burrow and looked around. He saw his father bounding back towards their home.

"Risky! Get your head back in that burrow until I'm there!"

Romi sensed Risky's excitement. She yelled out, "Hey! I want to see what's going on too!"

Romi started towards the opening but was nearly run over by Ruffy and Rambi in their zeal to do likewise. She hollered at them, "Hey! I should be next!"

Ruffy hardly looked back as he mumbled, "Just stay out of our way, Runt!"

Romi looked up at her mom, with a look that silently pleaded for maternal intercession. Rajina shook her head. She knew that it was not nice of Romi's big brothers, but she also knew that she could not always protect her dear runt. This was a safe place for her to start figuring out how to be the runty rabbit that she had been born as.

Rater was laughing at the bouncy excitement of the litter waiting for him at the entrance of the borrow. But he knew that this was a day of high danger along with the excitement. His young progeny would be the most vulnerable today. They were still learning how to tap their rabbitness, the very skills that they needed to make it through this day outside.

Rajina looked over at Rater. Together they knew how critical it would be to continue nurturing each young rabbit's gifts, so that they could survive in Mother Nature's drama.

The entire litter looked like they were trying to get out of the burrow hole all at once. Rajina giggled as she looked at seven wiggling cotton tails wedged together at the entrance. When Rumbly and Risky managed to pop out, the others just spilled out after them. Reya rolled onto the dew laden grass.

"Ahh... that's cold and wet!" she exclaimed.
Romi was the last one out. "Wow! That sun feels amazing! And it's so bright!"

Reya, Rowdy and Ruffy were quickly bounding to the other side of the yard.

"Wait a minute, you little rascals!" yelled Rater, "You don't even know where you're going!"

Rumbly and Risky yelled together, "Hey! Let's play chase!"

Their siblings all immediately joined in, loving the idea, realizing it would be so much more fun than in their little burrow.

Rambi said he would be it and the other bunnies tried to scatter in all directions. Romi realized very quickly how much slower she was than her siblings. They were quickly across the yard in the same amount of time it took her to just go a few paces. Rambi caught her in just a few strides.

"You're too easy to catch Romi. Maybe you should play another game," he called to her as he went full speed in the direction of Ruffy.

Romi pouted about what Rambi had just said. She was slowly realizing how her rabbit essence was very different from those of her siblings. She thought to herself, "Well, if I can't play the game, then I'll just see how I like these seedlings."

Soon she was head down, nibbling her way through the clover and grass shoots.

7
First and Fast Friends

*"Now here's someone who doesn't
make fun of me for being a runt."*

Romi and Reya had their heads submerged in the lush clump of chickweed that was flourishing on the rich soil of the otherwise empty flower bed.

Romi, talking with her mouth full, said to her sister, "You know, I'm really surprised how much I like the greens. I really thought that our mother's milk was the best food in the world, but now I see how much I still have to learn."

Reya laughed in agreement. "Yes, it's hard to believe that only hours ago the entire world we knew was our burrow. You know, I think I'm going to like becoming a big rabbit."

Romi's nosed twitched. "Do you smell that?"

Reya took an extra sniff in the thatch of the lawn. "Yes, I think that's where those other rodents often run through here. It doesn't smell like the mice that had their nest near our burrow though. Maybe it's the vole that father taught us about."

Rumbly came bounding in between them. "Hey, you two, did you see those birds up there? They're amazing!"

Reya looked up and around. As she eyed the vultures, she thought about the little rhyme her parents had taught her. She sung it aloud to Rumbly.
"If they glide, it's time to hide."

She looked skyward again. The warning in the rhyme seemed to match the situation. With a bit of shakiness in her voice, she told her sisters, "I think that one is gliding, maybe we should hide!"

Rumbly looked up and shook her head. "I don't think we need to worry. It's not really looking at us."

Romi wasn't so sure whether to trust her sister's explanation. She was ready to question it when the sound of other rabbit voices distracted her. She noticed another rabbit family exploring the other side of the garden lawn.

Romi remembered her parents telling them about Rebil and Redneg's family. She could feel her excitement building at the idea of finally getting to meet them.

Optimistic thoughts ran through her mind. "Maybe one of them will be my friend! Maybe they won't tease me for being a runt."

Her thoughts were interrupted by the sound of three small rabbits bounding towards her. She looked over at her mother for assurance. Rajina nodded that, indeed, it was okay.

The biggest one yelled out, "Hey! We're playing a game of hunt and hide. Do you want to join?"

Reya quickly responded, "Absolutely!"

Rumbly added, "Me, too!"

Romi was nervous. She was embarrassed at how poorly she did at the earlier game of chase, and didn't want to become the brunt of jokes to these potentially new friends.

Another of the approaching bunnies spoke up, "C'mon. It will be fun. You and I can hide together if you want."

Romi felt like this was a genuine invitation. Her delight at being included helped overcome her anxiety. "Thanks for asking me!"

She looked at the bunny who had extended the invitation and saw a pair of genuine, warm eyes. She quickly added, "I'm Romi."

The other rabbit stayed face to face with Romi, smiling broadly.

"I'm Rial," her new friend responded.

Rial sized Romi up, immediately sensing Romi's runtiness.

Her voice softened as she added, "I think we are going to be good friends."

Another rabbit quickly joined the conversation without need for an invitation. "I'm Rompy! Since I'm a most clever rabbit, I'll be it. Now, everyone go hide. I know I'll find you easily enough."

Romi and Rial ran off together. Rial spied a small nook by the garden bed and tried to jump in. Poking her head in, she squeaked, "This hole is a bit too small for me." Pulling her head back out, she said to Romi, "You're lucky because I think you'll fit in here."

"Hmm," thought Romi, "This must be what my parents were trying to tell me. That being a runt gave me some gifts that other rabbits didn't have. I can fit in smaller holes."

Romi wriggled in and then managed to turn herself around to look out.

Rial's face was now peering in. "You've found yourself a place that Rompy will never find."

Romi thought to herself, "Now here's someone who doesn't make fun of me for being a runt. She's right. I think we are going to be good friends."

Then to Rial, she said aloud, "Yup, it's part of my essence as a rabbit runt. Now you need to go find a place to hide before your brother gets here!"

Rial wasn't really sure what Romi meant by 'essence', but she looked around to find another good hiding place. What Rial did notice was that Romi's tone carried a hint of both confidence and humility. Rial compared that to the braggadocio attitude of her siblings. This was different. She thought that her new friend was indeed someone special.

After doing a quick survey around her, Rial turned and ran, hollering back to Romi, "Hey! I found a place!"

Rial hid behind an old crate that the humans had left by the garden. Rompy bounded by and quickly caught sight of Rial's tail, which was sticking out from behind the crate. Rompy was indeed clever. After confirming that he had found his sister, he assumed that Romi must be nearby. He playfully said aloud, "I wonder where that other rabbit could be hiding if she isn't with Rial? I'll probably never find her."

Romi started giggling at Rompy's feigned puzzlement. Within a few moments, Rompy's smirking face was at the entrance to the small niche in which Romi was snuggled.

The bunnies played another round of hunt and hide. Romi's siblings returned from their game, and the two families of young rabbits were enjoying getting to know each other. They followed the lead of the adult rabbits and started to look for food, listening closely to the advice that was offered to them. Rajina had pointed out a thick patch of starflower. Romi nibbled cautiously at first. She found it delicious, loving the new sensation of chewing her food, working the rabbit teeth that the Master had crafted for grinding up greens.

The sparseness of the early spring did not keep them from finding tender new shoots. The parents pointed out the crocus and tulip shoots that were near the house.

They cautioned their young explorers that going nearer to the house meant getting in sight of that big goofy brown dog that was apt to chase them. They shared that the bunnies would need to learn how soon they would need to run, as the large canine could actually run very fast when it wanted to, the parents instructed the bunnies to be extra cautious in timing when to start their escape. Despite the danger posed by the family dog, those tender flower shoots in the garden by the porch were worth the risk.

There was a special treat to which the rabbits looked forward to most. The humans would often throw vegetables into this big pile near the corner of the yard. The rabbits had no idea that the humans called this a compost pile. To them, it was a serendipitous supply of vegetables that was a welcome source of nourishment, especially during the barren winter months. The rabbits would be delighted at the various greens that would mysteriously arrive. Their favorite, of course, was when little bits of their most loved vegetable would be in the pile - carrots.

How the rabbits loved their carrots. The high sugar content delighted them. In many ways, carrots were rabbit candy. Like any candy, feasting only on carrots was not good for a rabbit to be as healthy and fast as it could be. So, while they loved them, they could not eat too many. Mother Nature, in her wisdom, had made it so that rabbits would not overindulge on carrots. She made it so that the carrots were hard to get out of the ground. Rabbits would often have to satisfy themselves with just the green tops, as this was what was most easily accessible. If they were to get the carrot roots, then it would have to be with the help of humans or other animals.

Romi jumped into the raised garden bed. Nuzzling around, she discovered some tender snap pea shoots. She passed the word to her siblings and new friends. The two litters were in awe of the wonders that the Master Craftsman had put in place.

It was only a matter of moments before the row, recently planted by the humans, was stripped clean by the rabbit families.

Romi heard some noise from the other side of the yard. Turning to look, she got to get her first visual of squirrels. She remembered that her parents had said squirrels were rodents who were herbivores like themselves. Romi took note of the family making its way out of their treetop home. The parents, whom she'd later learn were Squam and Squird, were teaching their own kittens, Squigs, Squags, Squank and Squim.

Romi hollered over to Rial, "Look, the squirrel family is coming out!"

Rial took note. She had heard about squirrels, but she never imagined them to look like what she was now seeing for the first time. Rial was fascinated by these neighbor mammals who had such a delicate way of moving along the tree branches, seemingly defying gravity. She was captivated by their tremendously bushy tails. She took great fascination with their paws that seemed to be so much more dexterous than her own. Rial watched as the family descended to the ground and were soon at work, finding what few seeds were still hiding beneath the leaf litter. She was intrigued how the father squirrel disappeared and then reappeared, holding a nut in his mouth which seemed too big to bite into.

Romi was calling over to Rial to join her in the chickweed patch, but Rial's fascination with the ways of the squirrel family distracted her from hearing. Romi went back to eating, wishing that Rial had joined her.

8
Sensing Essence

"...attuned to the rabbit gifts she did have, she was able to steer clear of danger, despite her runtiness."

Romi and her siblings were amazed by each day's transformations from being bunnies to acquiring their adult rabbitness. Their father never wasted an opportunity to reinforce how they needed to respect and nurture their rabbit gifts.

Romi loved how her father would often come up with playful ways to help them experiment with their rabbitness. Rater would sneak up on his young charges, so they would learn how powerful their ears really were. They could not only hear the tiniest of sounds but also locate where the sound was coming from. This would let them know which way to run away from danger.

Romi especially enjoyed that game. While the speed and strength games were difficult for her, she realized that her hearing was as good as any of her siblings. By being very attuned to the rabbit gifts she did have, she was able to steer clear of danger, despite her runtiness.

But it was not all fun and games. Romi and her siblings were now improving their survival skills and Rater was diligent in showing how to know when danger was near. One of the constant threats was Hank the hawk. Hank's territory was the sky above the grazing and gaming rabbits. His smooth flight was nearly silent. Thanks to Rater's stern teachings, Romi was learning how to attune her good rabbit hearing to even that.

Rajina joined Rater in the teaching. She pointed out how to spot when the sun would cast Hank's shadow onto the ground. She taught them that immediately after identifying the shadow they needed to perk up with eyes scanning wide and high. If they should sense any impending danger, they learned how to pass along an alarm to nearby rabbits as well.

The young rabbits learned that when the hawk would make its descent, they had to run as swiftly as they could. Since even their quickest dash was not as fast as the hawk, Rater and Rajina passed along what Mother Nature had taught them. If you can't outrun your predator, confuse them. So the rabbits would run zig-zaggy, making it hard for a diving hawk to catch.

Rajina and Rater were dedicated to this task of helping their progeny live within the guidelines of Mother Nature, using their essence of rabbitness, bestowed on them by the Master Craftsman, to the best of their ability.

Romi loved learning how to unleash her rabbit essence. She felt she learned a new marvel that the Master Craftsman had bestowed on rabbits with each passing day. Yet, she continued to be aware that as a runt, her gifts for speed and strength were not quite as good as the rest of the bunnies. Romi would need to rely on the rabbit gifts she did have if she was going to survive for long in this predator-prey arena.

When Romi wasn't learning from her parents, she was with Rial. The two were forging a tight friendship. Romi noticed that Rial's parents were not like her own.

For Romi and her siblings, ignoring or failing to grow into their rabbit gifts earned them a stern explanation on how these gifts were there for good and beautiful purposes. Romi's parents were emphatic that if and only if the rabbits treasured their essence and listened to Mother Nature, would they survive. They added that it wasn't just about survival, it was about being able to be the parents of the next generation.

But when she watched Rial or her siblings fail to appreciate or respect their rabbitness, their parents responded differently. They were reticent to admonish or correct their children when they found them not respecting their rabbit traits or the laws of Mother Nature. Romi found herself to be a bit envious of the liberties that Rial and her siblings seemed to have.

Romi continued to enjoy her lessons, but still wondered if her parents really understood how hard it was for her to be a runt. After all, they were not runts. But every time she used this as an excuse, her parents reminded her that she still was a rabbit, even if a runty rabbit. Rater and Rajina would stress how Romi needed to use the rabbit gifts that she did have, not to wish for the gifts that she did not have. Romi would frequently pout after these lectures, thinking that she could be just like the other rabbits. She wanted to ignore the obvious fact that she was a runt and live in her imagined world where she was as strong and fast as every other rabbit.

Romi looked across the field. She wondered what Rial was up to. Her friend seemed absolutely fascinated by various seeds that still remained on the ground. Rial even tried to pick up a nut that the squirrels had dropped in their escape from the big brown lab. She was now looking up at the tall tree, not in search of danger, but with a look of curiosity.

Romi was puzzled as to what her friend could be thinking. Surely Rial had to know that rabbits don't usually eat seeds and never eat nuts.

9
Parenting Paradox

*"This freedom that Sarty talked
about is really an invitation to a
chaotic hell."*

Redneg was very excited. After only hearing second hand what the new thinking was about, he was now going to be able to hear from the recognized authors of this new thinking. There was to a be special meeting that night and supposedly all animals were invited. To do this would mean to suspend the advice of Mother Nature so that both predator and prey could be together. Redneg was convinced that the predators would honor this advice because he assumed that all animals were equally excited about adopting this new thinking. The thought of learning more about freedom was all Redneg needed to cast off all the rabbit sense he had learned from his own parents.

He yelled over to Rebil, "All our young rabbits are safely back in their burrows. Pokey Possum will sound the alarm if any trouble comes nearby."

His mate was hesitant to travel across the field. This always meant exposing them to the tenacious talons of the Barred Owl or the hungry ferocity of the Fox. But, like Redneg, Rebil allowed her curiosity about this new thinking, and the freedom it promised, to fuel her courage.

"I'm ready to go," she told Redneg. Together they hurried over to make sure that Rajina and Rater were ready as well.

Rajina was coming back from talking with Pokey Possum and Squam. She was relying on her mammal neighbors to have extra eyes on her litter, from both the ground and the tree. Neither the possum nor the squirrel were the least bit interested in going to the meeting. Pokey had given his opinion that no one should play around with the guidance of Mother Nature. He also pointed out that the Master Craftsman had not made possums fast, ferocious or even all that clever, yet the possum race had been around just as long as any other furry animal. Squam had nodded in agreement, pointing out how squirrels were often seen as a bit spastic, but somehow that gift kept them surviving in the woods and even in human cities.

Rajina and Rater were still a bit nervous, even with the promise of watchfulness from their squirrel and possum friends. They were nervous because this new thinking seemed too good to be true. But out of friendship, and to show that they had open minds, they agreed to go.

As they made their way down the small grassy hill, Rater and Rajina instinctively stayed attuned to any sound or movement that could signal an oncoming predator. Redneg was almost chiding them for this, constantly saying that they'd need to get ready for the new thinking and the freedom that it promised. The four made their way to the edge of the small pond, in the valley, at the bottom of the hill. They saw other animals making their way as well. Despite the assurances that there would be no hunting tonight, Rater and Rajina were still cautious about trusting a hungry owl or fox who may be prowling nearby.

They looked into the pond from the small wall that bordered one edge. There on the big rock below they saw a frowning salamander and a haughty newt. On a nearby lily pad they saw a scowling frog who seemed to be perturbed at the arrival of the animals.

Asking around, they learned the names of these three amphibians. The newt, called Nishy, began to speak, an air of authority mixed with sadness in her tone.

"I know that most of you think that we were put here by the Master Craftsman. I know that most of you think that you need to live by the traits and talents that the Craftsman gave you, and to do that in accord with the laws that Mother Nature has laid down. But I say that we have come too far to still think there is a Master Craftsman. I say that he, or she, or it, is as good as dead. And, when the Master is dead, it means that we now have the freedom to be whatever we want. You are no longer held back by the definitions that were branded on you by the ideas of a Master Craftsman or Mother Nature. You can be your own masters."

The animals started to stir. Some of them found this a bit hard to accept while others were enticingly intrigued by the newt's somber ranting. Redneg relished the thought that he could be his own master.

Rater looked at Rajina. He whispered how he never really thought that he was some sort of slave to either the Master or the Mother, but rather a creature which they desired to live to his fullest, as his essence would accommodate.

Nishy continued, "Life is a self-assertive battle of the wills and it's always you against the world."

Redneg's excitement grew. He was ready to give a hoot in supportive agreement, but first looked at Rater with an expression that sought his neighbor's affirmation of the newt's message. But Rater was not affirming this message.

The newt put her head down, signaling that she had said what she wanted. Sarty slid his salamander body to a higher place on the rock.

He stood as tall as his sleek salamander frame would let him. "All of us need to get past this crazy idea of a great design by a Master Craftsman. We need to stop having a slave-like following to what some of you call the tune of Mother Nature. What many have been tricked into calling 'common sense' is not serving us well. Our existence, the fact that we are here now, is what defines us... not some crazy notion of the shape, size or type of animal we are. Because... let me ask you this... you prey... wouldn't you love to be free from being always pursued by predators?"

The predators had stayed at the edges of the crowd, sticking with their instincts. The salamander continued, acknowledging their presence. He knew that appealing to them would give him even more credibility.

"You predators... wouldn't you like to be free from the constant hunting... the long starving winters looking for prey that have burrowed themselves away?"

The prey animals were now a bit nervous, and Sarty knew that would make his words even more tempting.

"The most important value, the core of your existence is freedom. Not playing out a role that you never asked for. There is no pre-ordained path... the most important truth is that we exist and being conscious only of that existence is what will help set you free. Get rid of the idea of your essence... that which you thought defined you to be one type of animal or another. Toss aside the trap of binary thinking that defined you as predator or prey. Your freedom to use your existence is what will define you now, not some shape, form, muscle, or instinct that some Master Craftsman supposedly gave you. Face it, life is absurd. It has no meaning. It's all gonna just evaporate anyway. Your current existence is the only reality."

Rebil and Redneg, along with some of the other animals, listened with rapt attention to the salamander's words. They looked at each other with expressions that told the other that they thought these words were wise.

Not all found the message to their liking. Some animals bristled at the idea of going against what was so seemingly obvious. Shouldn't those who were built with an essence for speed believe that that meant running was part of their essence? Shouldn't those who had teeth to gnaw fibrous plants figure that meant they were designed to eat them? Shouldn't those who had claws that could dig put them to use making holes or finding roots?

Many of them thought that the words of these amphibians sounded a bit too good to be true. That the idea of pursuing freedom as the ultimate good seemed to be selfish at its core. It defied their basic purpose to go forth and multiply, to ensure that there would indeed be the next generation. And hadn't that ultimately selfless and long held view served all animals very well for, well, all of time? And were they to think that this great design was all just a result of some sort of accident?

Fucho purposely waited to allow the disagreement amongst the animals to move from a simmer to a boil. Then the frog spoke with his usual air of authority. "See this? All that stuff about Mother Nature and the Master Craftsman is just a way for some animals to maintain their dominance over other animals. It's time you all woke up to see that the whole story is nothing more than a power play by some animals."

Rater thought to himself, "If he, and everyone else, had to figure out who they were, wouldn't that mean he'd have to ignore a lot of obvious facts?"

He looked at his rabbit body and scratched his ears with his hind legs. "Yes, these are all very real, very tangible parts of me," he continued to think, "If I have to figure out who I am and it's not based on my biological reality, well, I'd be miserable. There's too many choices. It would force me to guess everyday whether I had chosen the correct, or best or even survivable version of who or what I am."

The notion made him feel sick. He could sense that following the amphibians' odd logic would lead to a lifetime of anxiety and angst.

Rater could see where this thinking would lead. He found himself silently giving himself a very different speech than the trio of amphibians before him. "This freedom that Sarty talked about is really an invitation to a chaotic hell. He thinks that freedom is doing what we want, rather than being free to do what we ought. He's inviting us to step away from where life makes sense to where nothing would make sense at all. And, that's the road to a deep danger, maybe even a danger to our very existence as rabbits." The thought made Rater's fur fluff out. The truth in his core sent an alarm, as Rater now began to see the deep threat that now was being preached.

On their way home up the hill, Redneg spoke about how clever these new ideas were. He was energized by the thought that with this freedom he could live outside the rules of some imaginary Mother Nature. That he and his family could be whatever they wanted, since he was now convinced that there really was no Master Craftsman's design to live by. He bantered on, echoing his favorite parts of the talks from the cold-blooded trio.

Rater listened and waited for a pause. He spoke thoughtfully, "I for one am not ready to assume that the Master Craftsman is dead or never existed. I see a resounding amount of truth, beauty and good in the world, and that needs a common source. And if we are all our own Craftsmen and our own Mothers, then where is the common good that we can live by? We end up more confused and at risk. Without having a way to look back at our essence, our identity is as flimsy as each passing moment that we exist in. That sounds like chaos to me. And when we give up on finding answers in the source of good, truth and beauty, it means that we will need to fill that void some other way. And, as far as I can figure, that would be the opposites of good, truth and beauty."

His fur again fluffed out, and his rabbit awareness sensed that if he continued to share his views, his words would not be well received by Redneg, who was still intoxicated from the amphibians' enticing utopian promise.

Rajina could see Rater's sense of alarm and noticed that he had stopped short. Continuing to walk along, she took up where her mate had left off. "I find it amusing that those three seemed to think because I respect what the Craftsman gave me and live in accord with the Mother, that somehow I am living in a fantasy world. Personally, I'm insulted by that. Would a fantasy provide me with a way to produce the next generation and prepare them for a world that, though seemingly difficult, is indeed the world for which we were made?"

Rajina stopped and turned and looked directly at Redneg. "I see a very careful design in the vast array of animals and their essences. For me, I don't see a slave driver. I do see that by abiding in the careful design of the Craftsman and the guidance of the Mother, I can live a full rabbit life and produce and prepare the next generation of rabbits. And it's in that second part that I find my purpose, and for rabbit-kind, it is the most important."

Redneg shook his head in a manner that revealed his lack of respect for Rajina's words. Rebil looked at her friend. Her eyes showed that she understood Rajina's perspective, but she continued to support Redneg's pursuit to help their friends adopt the new thinking.

Redneg put on an expression of a doting old mentor as he began to speak. Rater was amused at his friend's presumption, knowing that he had much more life experience than Redneg.

Redneg's voice took a pedantic tone, as if he was schooling a wayward student. "Rater, my friend, you need to open your mind. What in the world has the Master Craftsman ever really done for you? Why do you insist on thinking that he has your best interest in mind? Don't you want to be your own rabbit, freed from all the old conventions that you've been duped into living up to? Why, think of the possibilities if you just open your mind. You got to live in the moment, my friend, because how you exist says who you really are. I think you're being a bit stubborn there."

Rater nodded that he understood Redneg's invitation to see the new thinking. But he decided to say nothing. He had spoken his mind and if Redneg chose to continue trying to coerce him, that was Redneg's choice.

Redneg's whiskers wiggled. He misinterpreted Rater's silence. "I'm glad to see you thinking it all over. I'm sure that as you chew on the great words of the council, you'll come to see it their way. You know, the only way we'll make progress is thinking as the council recommends, and I for one am ready to support that transition. We need to get this new thinking underway, if not for us, at least for the next generation."

As the rabbit pairs separated to go to their own burrows, Rater shook his head. His fur was still a little fluffed out. "I just can't see how that new thinking can lead to anything good in the long term. I think it will more likely lead to a bunch of confused rabbits, and confused rabbits don't last too long in our world, whether it's old or new."

Rajina nodded. "As if parenting wasn't hard enough already. We work hard to teach them how to protect themselves against the predators of their bodies. Now we have to teach them how to be strong against these predators of their minds."

She stepped towards the father of her litter and gave him a little nuzzle with her nose, showing him they were in this together.

10

Doubts and Dreams

---

*"The gecko knew that he only needed
one more myth, cloaked in what
sounded like truth, to pull his victim
into a deadly doubt."*

R omi was still trying to catch her breath.

She had just finished zig zagging around the yard. It seems that the big brown lab had decided it wanted her as a playmate when it realized that this runt was a catchable rabbit.

Romi turned towards her friend, who had come up alongside her. "I can't believe that you made enough noise to distract that goofy dog. I thought I was a goner when everyone ran and I couldn't keep up."

Romi felt like her heart was going to jump out of her chest from the excitement of the dangerous chase, combined with the realization of what her friend had just done for her.

She tried to recall what had happened. While running from the canine she had heard Rial making a ruckus under the azalea bush. It must have been sufficiently distracting since the lab got sidetracked from its pursuit of her. The dog's pouncing investigation nearly ruined the azalea and earned it a call into the house by the humans.

Romi moved closer to Rial. "I can't believe that you put yourself in danger to get that dog to stop chasing me. You're a true friend, Rial."

Rial acknowledged Romi's appreciation with a calm smile. "Well, I don't know about you, but that little episode made me very hungry. Let's see what we can find over here."

The two skipped over towards the box gardens.

Romi's nuzzled her nose deep into the creeping Charlie, looking for the tenderest young portions of the plant. She was startled when a gecko, in hot pursuit of a cricket, stopped short in front of her. As the cricket made a getaway, the gecko glared at Romi.

"You made me miss that cricket!" he hissed.

Romi recognized the pursuer. It was Gabbadon, the gecko. She had seen him at various dark corners of the garden boxes.

The gecko, feigning to be irritated, continued. "Well…if it isn't Romi. Your clumsy eating caused me to miss my afternoon snack."

Romi blurted out an apology, trying to recover from being startled herself by the gecko's rash reaction.

Rial noticed Romi having a conversation and ambled over to her friend.

Gabbadon continued as if Rial wasn't there, "You know, Romi, you're a little runt because the Master Craftsman doesn't like you. You need to start realizing that you don't have stay a runt. You know, if you believe it, you can make that happen. You don't have to accept what the Master Craftsman and Mother Nature put in place. Look at me… I can change my colors so that I can avoid being seen by my predators, but what's really cool is that I can hide from those I want to eat."

Gabbadon had long ago taken credit for being his own creator. He had already deluded himself into believing that his gecko ability to change colors was his own doing. He shared his distorted view of reality on his gullible listeners. "The fact that I can change is proof that we don't have to be what the Master Craftsman intended."

Romi and Rial were a bit taken aback by this impromptu lecture from Gabbadon. But the gecko's clever seduction got them both thinking.

For Romi, the idea that she could think her way out of being a runt was very appealing. That would make sense. Why in the world would the Master Craftsman have given her this burden of being the slowest bunny? Romi shook her head, her ears flopping back and forth. The gecko's invitation stood in stark contrast with the advice her parents of often repeated. "Be who you are and be that well. Don't be who you aren't."

Romi reflected on her parents' words, but the gecko's deceit fed her ego. She thought to herself. "But what if I don't like who I am, a runt."

Gabbadon's tempting invitation was similarly enticing to Rial. It made sense. Why not be who she wanted to be rather than what the Master Craftsman had made her to be? She began to see herself as trapped in her rabbit body. Gabbadon seemed to be pointing to a way to escape that trap.

The wily master of disguise smiled as he saw his words play on the sensibilities of the young rabbits. Gabbadon knew that if he could get them doubting the goodness of Mother Nature, it would be the first step on their slide into his lair of deception.

Gabbadon was especially excited to see how his words affected Rial. He had watched this young rabbit's fascination with the squirrels. His trio of friends had already brought her parents into the new thinking, so the field was fertile for fomenting division amongst the rabbit families.

Gabbadon noted the look on Rial's face. The young bunny's eyes revealed her thoughts. The gecko knew that he only needed one more myth, cloaked in what sounded like truth, to pull the his victim into a deadly doubt.

He put on a soft smile, feigning an attitude of caring. "You can't trust that Mother Nature or Master Craftsman have what's best for you in mind. You need to make your own truth."

11

Who Am I

"You have rabbitness, not
squirrelliness.
I can see that."

The rabbit families were out foraging. The sun was warm, and they enjoyed many tender shoots that had been coaxed to pop their heads above the earth.

Risky, ever the explorer, had discovered a pile of discarded human goodies. It included a mound of carrots that were not all that fresh, but in the scarcity of early spring foods, were a great find. He yelled out a message to the rest of the rabbit crowd. They all happily scampered towards the pile.

Rajina and Rater signaled caution to their young family. They had learned that humans knew rabbits liked carrots. They had also learned that humans sometimes put this food in places to trap a rabbit in, and then that rabbit would never be seen again.

Romi and Rial were close by as Rajina and Rater put out the call that it was safe. Romi was excited since this meant that for once she'd be the first to the pile. The two bounded over the garden boxes towards the orange treasures.

Romi was pleased with herself as she was able eat some carrots before the rest of siblings and friends arrived. She saw a very old, but still delicious, carrot that had rolled into the grass. She pointed it out to Rial.

Rial approached the carrot with a bit of curiosity. She studied it. Romi was amused at how much thought her friend was putting into the carrot. Rial scowled at the sweet delicacy before her. She walked away with a look of indifference, maybe even contempt.

Romi continued to nibble with gusto on the sweet root. But she was distracted by her friend's odd behavior. Rabbits never walked away from a carrot. She wondered if Rial still thought it was a bit of a trap.

"If you don't grab that carrot now, one of my brothers will be scarfing it up before you know it!" Romi joked in a good-natured way.

Rial did not seem to care.

Romi continued, after getting another mouthful of carrot, "What's wrong? Is that one bad?"

Looking at her friend, Rial announced with a feigned air of assuredness, "I don't like carrots."

Romi thought she was kidding and giggled a little.

Rial clearly did not like Romi's reaction.

Romi wasn't sure how to respond at this point. Surely Rial could not have meant what she said.

Romi wanted her friend to get some of the feast before it was gone. "Well, that's a surprise, but there are other goodies in the pile as well. The humans have put all sorts of neat stuff in here."

Rial stood up on her hind legs, without even bothering to investigate what Romi was inviting her to eat.

"I don't like carrots, and I don't like that lettuce or that broccoli either."

Romi stopped chewing. Rial's serious tone had caught the attention of the other compost pile foraging rabbits as well.

Rial continued, "I don't really like any of the greens that rabbits eat. I prefer nuts and seeds. I've figured out that I'm not really a rabbit. I'm a squirrel."

At first, Romi didn't know how to react. She sort of thought that Rial was just pretending, as all bunnies like to do, when they still have much to learn about their rabbitness. Why, just yesterday, Rowdy and Ruffy were pretending to be foxes and chasing the other bunnies.

But this was different.

Romi hopped closer to Rial. The other rabbits, realizing that Romi had the situation under control, went back to the tasty business at hand.

Romi looked at Rial, who by now had returned to all fours.

"Rial, I don't understand. Are you playing around? Is this a new game?"
Rial looked away thoughtfully, avoiding Romi's eyes. "My parents told us that we need to figure out who we are. I figured out that I'm a squirrel. A squirrel trapped in a rabbit's body."

Romi's back leg reached around to scratch her ear.

Rial continued, "I prefer to eat nuts and seeds. And I believe that I would be happier living in the trees."

Romi was conflicted. She felt sad but wondered if she was somehow supposed to be happy for her friend. Romi challenged Rial, "Ok, Rial, I've seen you try to eat the nuts and seeds and I've watched you try to climb a tree. My mother taught us that nuts and seeds, even if we could chew them, are really bad for rabbits. Aren't you afraid of getting sick?"

Rial didn't answer.

Romi tried another tactic. "Well, why do you think you're a squirrel? I mean, all you know is what you've seen. You don't have any squirrel essence... you're not squirrelly. You have rabbitness, not squirelliness. I can see that."

Rial looked wistfully past Romi. "I just know I'm supposed to be a squirrel. I really like how squirrels live.

They get to fly around in the tree tops, they can hold their food in their hands."

Romi nodded. "Yes, I know that all looks cool, but..."

At this point, Romi was confused. She didn't finish her statement because she didn't even know what to think herself. Was Rial right? Could Rial really be a squirrel? If that were true, then maybe what Gabbadon had said was really true as well. And if so, maybe that meant that she was not actually a runty rabbit, but whatever rabbit she wanted herself to be. Now that was a tempting thought.

P. F. Armstrong

12

A Dream Dared

---

*"All I have to do is break free from
the runty prison that the Master put
me in."*

The sun had brought unusual warmth to the day. The young rabbits were able to wander a bit further from their burrow, but still under the careful eyes of their parents.

Romi found herself trailing behind her siblings in their romps to discover new patches of green and tender shoots. Feelings of envy started to creep into her consciousness. Feelings of not being a worthy rabbit played on her mind. She started to hate that she was the runt and resented being the one left behind. Romi wondered why a Master Craftsman would ever have made a runt in the first place. It seemed like he never really wanted her to be born at all. She started to feel a self-righteous anger at the role to which the Master Craftsman had shackled her.

Gabbadon's words echoed in her mind. His crafty logic moved the ideas from being curiously tempting to downright persuasive.

Romi thought to herself, "Maybe, I really could just be a normal rabbit. All I have to do is break free from the runty prison that the Master put me in. If I'm a regular rabbit in my mind, then that is how I can exist. I just need to act like a regular rabbit."

She saw that the others had settled into a particularly luscious patch of clover and hopped over to join the feast.

A shadow passed over the grazing family. Rater's head popped up out of the clover. His rabbit eyes scanned with their wide range of vision. His rabbit ears tuned to listen well to the tiniest of sounds. He noticed an eerie silencing of avian songs, and that hush of music was an alarming sound to this rabbit.

Rater made a sudden motion that quickly alerted the grass nibbling clan, who all became tense. The muscles in their hind legs filled with rabbit hormones, setting them ready to spring into action. The shadow continued to pass over them.

Rater's rabbit instincts triggered the awareness that this was an impending attack from Hank the hawk. The rabbit father scurried around, passing along what he realized. His offspring, whose instincts were still being honed, obeyed their father's warnings. They scattered in different directions. Romi and her siblings all began to run in seemingly random zig zag patterns.

Hank was delighted with what he saw on the ground. Lots of rabbits. Surely one will be an easy catch. He saw the rabbits starting to scatter. "Those scared songbirds have stopped singing!" Hank thought to himself.

He scanned what was now an empty horizon. The singing nuisances had all cleverly hidden themselves from his gaze. The sharp-eyed raptor looked down on the scampering band of rabbits and bunnies.

"Well, I'll be. Look at Mr. Pokey Bunny," he whispered to himself, as he looked down on Romi. "I can almost taste this one already." With one smooth tip into the wind to mask his scent and sound, Hank started his descent.

Romi knew from her father how to scatter and find a place to hide. But her mind was full of thoughts about how she hated being considered a runt. She kept seeing herself as a regular rabbit. The ego driven image swelled her pride to the point that she momentarily ignored all the obvious evidence of her runtiness.

The fantasy in her mind betrayed all the good advice her parents had given her. Romi pictured herself as a non-runty rabbit, convincing herself that she could now run as fast as her siblings.

After all, couldn't she just decide for herself who she was? Couldn't she just will herself out of the runtiness? Gabbadon had told her so. The new thinking promised her a freedom from what the Master had shackled her to.

Romi deluded herself into thinking that she was running like the others. She took a zig here and a zag there. The other bunnies were quickly outpacing her, but she didn't let that change her mind.

Several others had run past a hole at the bottom of the white fence post, since it was too small to hide in. Romi knew that she would fit in that hole, but she did not want to rely on her runtiness. Swelling with pride, she now fully believed that she was a regular rabbit.

She ran past the small hole.
Hank's descent speed increased. He smiled, beginning to close the gap on his intended victim.

Rater was puzzled when Romi passed by the perfectly good hiding spot.

He wondered to himself, "Hasn't she realized that she's probably the intended target for Hank's talons?"

The scattering rabbits had attracted the attention of the goofy brown lab, who happened to be sleeping nearby. Pretending to be ready for the hunt, the dog took note of the hawk closing in. In what was more play than pursuit, he bounded across the lawn, barking skyward, comically thinking he could leap at the descending hawk.

Hank noticed the brown dog closing in on his prey. The dog's head turned in his direction, making a terrible racket. Hank had seen this behavior before and was always confused about the intentions of the canine. But the hawk knew better than to dismiss the strange scenario. Though the dog's pursuit was half-hearted, it was enough to put doubt into Hank's mind.

He thought, 'that crazy dog... he just ruined it!'
Hank slightly adjusted his wingtips and his rapid descent was translated into a circling arc, back skyward and over the houses.

Romi's father saw the flight change of the avian predator. He was thankful for the interruption by the goofy lab. Rater realized that even in the continual drama of predator and prey, sometimes there seemed to be random luck. His relief at Romi's escape allowed him to be amused at the behavior of that bulky dog. Still, he never understood the animal that lived in the house with the humans. Why in the world would it chase a bird it could never catch? Regardless, the silly behavior of the dog had resulted in saving his dear Romi from being Hank's next meal.

Romi had heard the dog barking, but did not see it chasing the hawk. All Romi saw was Hank soaring away from her, getting higher in the air.

Pride swelled inside her and she bragged to herself, "I did it! I'm a regular rabbit! I'm not a runt!"

Rater bounded over to Romi. "I am so glad you're still here! My heart stopped when I saw that the hawk had every intention and opportunity to snag you. By some gift of Mother Nature that dog interrupted the hawk's plan."

His tone quickly changed from grateful relief to lecturing father though. "But Romi, why in the world did you not go into that small hole?"

Romi was stunned. Why was her father upset? She thought he'd be proud of her.

Her adrenaline started to subside. In its place, a sense of self-serving righteousness grew, feeding on her pride.

She thought to herself, "Hadn't she just proven that she didn't need to be the runt that she was born as?"

Her own pride influenced her response and she burst out, "Because I believe I don't have to be the runt anymore! And I think I just proved that"

Rater, who was now a fully fluffed out rabbit, cut her off with a booming "You're wrong!"

Rater saw what was either hurt or anger in his young daughter's eyes. He paused enough to let his heart slow down. He made a silent thanks to whatever reason he had not lost his precious progeny. The moment of gratitude restored his sense of perspective.

Now able to speak calmly, he spoke to his daughter. "Romi, I dearly love you. Your mom and I are helping you to be the best rabbit you can be, and that includes being the best runt you can be. But we cannot ignore the biological reality here. Our job, as your parents, is to help you be the best version of yourself based on what the Master Craftsman has given you. And just then, it would have served you well to duck into that small hole... even if it came at the cost of your pride."

The other rabbits were slowly coming back from their scattered escape routes. They were surprised that all of them were still there. They knew that life as prey is filled with days when predators win and thanked the Craftsman for their gifts of rabbitness that gave them the ability to escape as often as they did.

Her father's candid disapproval of her actions stung her pride and she looked to find solace in the cunning words of Gabbadon. Romi so wanted to think that the Craftsman hated her and made her a runt just to be mean. She wanted to think that she knew better than the Craftsman, better than her father.

Nearby rabbits started to reappear, evidence of how much further they had run. Shadowed against the clouds, she saw Hank, still circling in the distance. The reality of how she was not his midday meal finally replaced her illusion of being her own hero. She began to reflexively twitch and lowered her eyes, hoping her father wouldn't see.

But as she did, she saw that he was not only still fluffed up, but was also twitching. Instead of seeing a disciplinarian against whom she had victoriously rebelled, she saw a loving parent whose caring advice she had foolishly discarded.

Romi put her head down. In her mind, she could hear the gecko's words. They no longer sounded like an answer, as the shroud of their deceitfulness was pulled back. The gecko had fed her an illusion of life being about fun and freedom. She had mistakenly thought that meant she didn't need what sounded like harsh advice from her parents. But her father was proof that parental love is not the same as being tolerant. Sometimes, it may not even sound that tender.

Her parents' care for her was real. Their insistence to be what the Craftsman made her to be was not senseless discipline or overbearing parenting. It was genuine parental love, a love that sought to keep her on a path of real truth.

Romi lifted her head and looked at her father. She now better understood that love which bestowed on her real truth, so that she could live in the beautiful ways intended by the Craftsman.

She moved closer and nodded her head. Rater accepted her nuzzle, a sign that she was both apologetic and now knew better. He signaled her towards a patch of clover.

Meanwhile, Hank did a slow circle high above the rabbits. He saw the dog wagging its tail, seemingly proud even though its chase had been futile. The hawk pouted as he glided on the wind current towards an old walnut tree. He tried cheering himself up, hoping that maybe he'd find an unsuspecting squirrel.

13
Call to Duty

"I fear that I have not lived up to the challenge."

Rajina had heard the ruckus that ensued from Romi's close encounter with tragedy. She peered out from the burrow. Rater was coming towards her with his ears back and his fur still fluffed out. She knew that her mate was upset.

Before she could even ask what had happened, Rater exploded into a rant.

"You know, Rajina, we've raised three other litters of bunnies and have been able to teach them how to survive as prey in this predator filled world. But I really wonder about what is going on now."

The rabbit father scratched his ear with his hind leg, as if that would unlock the confusion that currently clouded his thoughts. He looked over at the mother of his litter.
Rater stopped scratching and continued, "Our daughter had an incredibly close call just now. She decided to believe the crazy idea that she was not a runt and thought she'd be able to outrun Hank the hawk. She ran past some very good little runt sized escape holes. I thought she was a goner. It was only because of the crazy brown lab that we still have her."

Rajina took a deep breath, trying to come to grips with what Rater had just shared. She thought she'd get more details as Rater began to speak, but the look in his eyes made her quickly realize that he had something even more important to say.

Rater took a deep breath and continued, "I thought that we had instilled in our children to respect the essence that they have been given by the Master Craftsman, and to use that essence in concert with the guidance of Mother Nature. We've done that successfully with our other three litters. I know that Rebil and Redneg don't seem to emphasize this as much as we do, and I don't know what to think about Rial's influence on Romi."

Rater's fur slowly started to smooth back down, as dismay and confusion weighed on his heart. "I used to think that all creature parents knew this, how to be truly loving parents in the sacred duty of raising our young. I thought we all knew that we live in a good world, though not an easy one. I thought we knew that to survive and produce the next generation we have to live up to and into our essence. And it seems so obvious that ignoring what we were created to be makes us much easier prey. That's been a constant since the dawn of time."

Rater idly nibbled at some nearby starflower, more out of a need to stop and think than out of hunger.

Rajina nodded, showing that she was clearly following where his thoughts were going. Her silence signaled that she was open to hear more.

Rater finished nibbling. His ears were still back, but the meager few bites had seemed to nourish his resolve. He spoke with a tinge of righteous anger, as fur began to fluff again.

"You and I both know that our job is to prepare them to be rabbits who can survive, rabbits who will go forth and multiply. But I'm scared that what you and I, and all other creatures before us, took as our sacred duty is now being questioned."

Rater paused, twitching one ear.

"I really think that the near-death experience today of our dear Romi was because she started to think that she could ignore her essence. I worry that she has fallen prey to something more dangerous than that hawk... I'm talking about that new thinking."

Rater's head dropped, his eyes going from anger to sadness. "I really worry that our job as parents has gotten a lot harder, and I fear that I have not lived up to the challenge."

Rajina hopped alongside the brave rabbit she was happy to have as her mate, as she began to respond, "Rater, you know that I completely agree with you." Rajina started to pace a little. "I believe that we are being called to a higher duty than just teaching our young ones how to use their essence to thrive as rabbits, to survive as prey.

We see how Rebil and Redneg have tossed aside the wisdom of ages, and how that has allowed what may have been a passing fantasy to become a dangerous illusion for some of their litter. You know, I wonder whether we were too polite in our conversations with them. I know that we have had many spirited discussions, but I always felt like I had to tolerate their position, even as I strongly believed it to be dangerous. I found myself scared to love them enough to tell them that they were stepping away from both the laws of nature and the inherent logic of creation. And you and I both now know that to do that was to flirt with death in an unnecessary, unnatural way."

Rajina slumped a bit as she continued, "So, yes, I agree with you, my dear Rater. I fear that I have not met the challenge on both ends, in both helping our friends to stay on Mother Nature's path and to strengthen our children from the temptation to leave that path."

She came alongside the emotionally exhausted father. "What I fear, Rater, is that this new thinking will gradually destroy the very fabric of our species, sowing a confusion about how to live into and up to our essence. To me, that new thinking, with its basis in what exists in the moment, is like a sweet tasting yet poisonous plant. In the moment, as it did with Romi, the new thinking sates our ego's appetite, but its toxicity slowly destroys being true to our real essence, our real purpose as creatures."

Rajina surveyed the area around them, and as her eyes and ears took in their world, she continued, "We need to stay strong in our belief. To alienate our offspring's alliance from the ways of Mother Nature would be to disregard the sacredness of our duty as parents."

Rajina looked at Rater. His ears stood upright. Looking out across the lawn, he thought aloud, "I believe that we have a higher call to duty."

14
My Name Is

---

*"Don't be giving me that nonsense
about how my rabbit body must mean
I'm a rabbit."*

The spring days were getting longer and longer. The rabbits were finding more and more tender shoots popping up from the ground. The chickweed was deliciously thick, and a rabbit could spend all day nibbling way.

Romi found what she thought was an especially delicious patch.

"Hey Rial, you should come over and taste this. It's really sweet!"

Rial stood on her hind legs. "Call me Squipples. My name is Squipples now."

Romi's big rabbit ears clearly heard what Rial had said, but her mind failed to make sense of it.

Romi pulled her head high above the chickweed, and without finishing chewing, queried back, "What did you say, Rial? Something about ripples?"

Rial came back up on her hind legs. "You must start calling me by my new name. It's Squipples!"

Romi shook her head. "But you're Rial. And besides, Squipples is a squirrel name."

She let the strange name roll around in her head for a moment, and then added, "It's even hard for rabbits to pronounce!"

Rial got upset. "Why are you making such a big deal about this? Why are you refusing to be my friend and call me Squipples? And of course it's a squirrel name. You know that I identify myself as a squirrel now."

Romi was torn.

"But Rial... er, I mean... Squipples, I am your friend. Ok. I'll try to call you Squipples, but when I see you I really think..."

Rial cut her off. "Don't be giving me that nonsense about how my rabbit body must mean I'm a rabbit. I get to decide what and who I am, and I'm a squirrel!"

Romi remained confused and torn, not wanting to continue this dangerous game. She did want to be a good friend. Actually, she wanted to be a real friend, and she knew that real friends help to keep their friends safe. She knew that real friends don't lie, even if the lie supports a fantasy the friend is entertaining. It was becoming more and more clear to Romi that Rial's nut eating and tree climbing habits were not healthy.

Romi also thought about her own desire to be a non-runty rabbit, and how all that desire was still powerless to take away her runtiness. Not knowing what else to do, she pretended to be more interested in the chickweed and put her head back down. Rial hopped away in a huff, joining the others in a game of chase.

In the game, Ruffy was apparently it. Rial attempted to escape by climbing a tree, but that did not end well.

"You're now it, Rial!" Ruffy exclaimed as he tagged her.

"I'm Squipples! I told you that!" Rial screamed back.

Ruffy just shook his head and rambled away. But not fast enough. Redneg had heard the exchange. He went racing after the unsuspecting Ruffy.

"You're not respecting who she is!" He screamed at Ruffy.

Ruffy was both shocked and scared by the sudden raucous reprimand. So, Ruffy did what rabbits do best. He ran off. He was confused about whether to be embarrassed, angered or upset.

Rajina saw what had happened. She kept these encounters in her heart, contemplating how to continue to love all rabbits. She remained convinced that her calling from Mother Nature was to train the young rabbits to grow in their rabbitness, and was very concerned that Rial, in her pursuit to be squirrelly, would actually stunt her very own rabbitness. Rajina knew that as prey, they needed every bit of rabbitness they had to stay clear of danger.

Romi hopped over to be close to her mother. "Mother, I'm concerned. Rial wants to have a squirrel name. She's always trying to climb trees, and gets hurt falling out. She's even trying to rub her ears to make them smaller. And what's really weird is that she's trying to give herself a tail! But thankfully, I don't think her ideas will work."

"Yes, I see that too, Romi. And I'm concerned as well." Rajina thought of what she had heard at the council meeting. Her ears slanted back, and in a barely audible whisper, added, "Actually, I'm very concerned."

Redneg gathered his young rabbits and signaled for them to meet at the other end of the yard.

He stood on his hind legs. "Look! You guys are not prisoners of the Master or the Mother. You can be whatever you want to be. You all should figure what and who you are. We should all admire Squipples' courage."

Rompy, who was always the last one home in the evening, pondered his father's words. "Maybe, I'm really nocturnal by nature. And I'm a most clever chaser when we play tag..."

Rompy unconsciously scratched his ear with his hind leg. "Hmm. I must be a fox!"

Rompy's mind, fertilized by the manure of the new thinking, was growing doubts. He began to confuse imagination with what was true creature instinct. He misinterpreted his playful pursuit of mice with the predator pursuit of foxes. He slowly started to craft a new version of himself. Rompy figured this self-formed image must constitute who he really was, regardless of the realities of his rabbit physiology.

P. F. Armstrong

15
Viral Guile

---

*"… his trap had worked. He had
sown the confusion."*

Rompy and Rial were heading out to forage.

Rial told Rompy, "I'm going to head over to the pine trees and see if there are any pine nuts left in the cones. I'm having a hard time finding any."

Rompy looked at his sister with a mix of puzzlement and admiration. "Rial, I've been wanting to ask you. Where or how did you get the courage to know it was time to speak up about being a squirrel?"

Rial stopped and answered, "Some was from our father, but mostly it was that gecko, Gabbadon, who helped me straighten out my thoughts."

Rompy thought about that for a minute, mumbling aloud. "Hmm, maybe I should stop by and see him myself."

Rial nodded in approval, and with words that belied more than she realized, added, "It can't hurt."

The animal kingdom has many channels of communication and the conversation got passed along through the various critters. It was not long before it came to Gabbadon. He smiled inwardly, his mind already scheming how to make the deception complete.

Rompy shyly hopped to where Gabbadon was pretending to be hunting.
"Hey, Gabbadon..."

Gabbadon acted startled and surprised. "My goodness, how did you manage to sneak up on me like that? Why, for a rabbit you are quite stealthy... a clever stalker!"

Rompy heard the words and smiled. Maybe the gecko was right. Maybe he was not really a rabbit at all, but a fox... his nocturnal yearnings, his fascination to chase mice and now, his ability to be so stealthy were all pointing to what he must really be.

Gabbadon could see the thoughts playing in Rompy's mind. "Well, my good friend, you certainly look like a rabbit. But that's just an outward appearance, and who would know better than me that outward appearances can be deceiving... maybe not just to others but even to ourselves."

The gecko delivered his line in a way that sounded like he had just thought of it rather than the calculated delusion that he had been rehearsing for a while now.

Rompy chimed in, "You know, Gabbadon, you may be onto something. My parents told me that I can be whatever I want. I feel trapped in this rabbit body... but didn't the Master Craftsman make me a rabbit?

Gabbadon was ready for this line of thinking. "You know, Rompy, that you can't really trust that Master Craftsman. If he really cared about you, he'd let you be whatever you want to be."

Camouflaging himself in false empathy, the gecko spoke with an artificial thoughtfulness, "Sometimes, I really wonder if the Master Craftsman has just left altogether." He paused and cast a glance at the rabbit to make sure his words were causing the doubt he intended. Picking up the same tone, he continued, "I don't know, maybe he's already dead and left Mother Nature here to keep his work going."

The gecko made sure his deceit was still cleverly disguised as caring. "You know, I think that's it. The Craftsman has gone away and Mother Nature has more than she can handle. But, as your cleverness indicates, you are perfectly able to figure life out as you want."

Rompy did not know what to think and Gabbadon noticed the look of confusion on the little rabbit's face. He loved a confused mind, one that was ready to let go of truth and buy into his lie. His words had achieved their intent. He had baited the snare that would make the rabbit his.

Rompy did not see the trap that he was falling into. His mind was now infected with the amphibian's alluring temptations to be his own craftsman. The gecko's logic was tantalizingly believable and Rompy was now sure that the Craftsman either didn't really care or didn't exist. This meant that the rabbit was free to be what he wanted. He'd be free to be the fox he imagined he was supposed to be. The thought brought a certain pride fed happiness. Yet, he wasn't really sure he was happy.

The clever gecko pretended to be in pursuit of a damselfly and scampered away. He knew that his trap had worked. He had sown the confusion. The little rabbit's parents would allow that confusion to take root along with their own belief in what the cold-blooded council had spread.

Gabbadon giggled nefariously to himself as he thought how clever he was to lead others away from the works of the Craftsman and the ways of the Mother. In their wayward walk away from what was true, beautiful and good, he would lead them into confusion, ugliness and despair. And to him, that was a misery he loved the company of.

16
Deception Gets Protection

---

*"It's time you all woke up to the
reality that we aren't trapped…"*

Rompy thought about what the gecko had said before darting off in pursuit of its prey. The little rabbit had not realized the cleverness of the gecko's trap. By not actually telling the rabbit to be a fox, the guileful gecko had fed Rompy a piece of temptation disguised as freedom. He knew that if Rompy believed he could freely choose a life other than what the Craftsman had given, the rabbit would have a sense of being his own craftsman. And that little taste of power would tantalize him into thinking this choice was the first step to being free. While this was the oldest deceit in all of time, it continued to contain its cruel potency.

By the end of the week, Rompy was ready to tell his parents and siblings. They were all in the clover, still

moist from the morning dew. Talking with his mouth full, Rompy stood as tall as his rabbit legs would allow.
"I've finally realized why I like to prowl around and why I like to stay out at night more than in the day."

His siblings and parents looked up, as they all continued chewing their grassy breakfast.

Rompy saw he had their attention. "I realized that I am a fox trapped in a rabbit's body."

Rispy sighed, "Good grief! Not you too!"

Redneg immediately hopped over to Rispy. "What do you mean by that?! It's time you woke up and realized that Rial and Rompy are finally free to be who they want to be. You should be ashamed of yourself for not celebrating your brother's brave decision!"

Rispy put her head down to escape the condemning glare of her father.

Rompy then declared, "And my name is Foreal."

Rebil went over to her son. "Ah... Foreal. It has a good ring to it. So does this mean you'll need to sleep all day so you can prowl all night?"

Rompy smiled at his mother's calm acceptance of his news. He bounded across the yard to where Romi and her siblings were playing around the garden boxes.

"Hey everyone," he hollered, "You all need to know that I'm not really a rabbit. I'm a fox. You should call me by my new name, Foreal."

Romi's heart ached. She knew better than to say anything and pretended to be distracted by some movement in the chives.

Ruffy looked up at Rompy. "Really, a fox?"

Thinking that Rompy was just playing some sort of new game, he continued, "Well, Rompy, I'm busy eating. We can play later, but this time I want to be the chaser."

Rompy felt a surge of anger. "You're not listening, Ruffy! I said I'm a fox, and you need to call me Foreal!"

His voice was loud enough for Redneg to hear. The indignant father was soon at the garden boxes.

"What's going on here?"

Rompy whined that Ruffy was not calling him by his new name.

Redneg was now yelling at Ruffy, but his loud voice made it clear that this mandate was for the entire clan before him.

"You need to start respecting the freedom of others to choose for themselves. It's time you all woke up to the reality that we aren't trapped into what that fairy tale you call the Master Craftsman dumped on us."

Then, glaring at Ruffy, he snarled, "and if you or your siblings don't start calling him Foreal, I'll be taking this to the council and see what they think."

Romi and her siblings stopped chewing and stared at each other, feeling pangs of guilt. They had been taught to respect their elders, but this reprimand from Redneg made them feel sick and confused. The deep truths inside of them rebelled at this glaring denial of the Craftsman's careful design and Mother Nature's rules. They were not sure what Redneg's threat really meant, but they had heard some crazy stories from rabbits who had left areas where the council's thinking was becoming more accepted.

Rater decided that he needed to step in. He bounced over and invited Redneg to go with him to explore a patch of budding tulips.

Rater began, "I hear that Rompy is calling himself a fox and that his new name is Foreal. Is that true?"

Redneg, still a bit hot from the earlier encounter, tried to calm himself. "Yes, it is very true. And your family has got to start accepting that..."

Redneg paused, his ears tipped back and his eyes narrow, showing his increasing impatience with his neighbor's stiff resistance. He continued in a more demanding tone, "No, they should not just accept it, they should celebrate it. This is a new freedom!"

Rater took a deep breath. "I see, but then again, I don't. I don't really understand what this new freedom will lead to. I speak for myself, but I think I also speak for the joyfully successful generations of rabbits before me. Actually, I already see myself as free. I see that by following Mother Nature and living in the essence given by the Craftsman, I am best able to pursue my purpose to go forth and multiply. And from that, free to fulfill my fatherly purpose to love my offspring, teaching them how to live with the essence they've been given.

Redneg was shaking his head. "See there, Rater. That's your problem. You are so stuck in your old thinking that you can't even recognize yourself as trapped."

Rater stopped long enough to show Redneg where the tulips were starting to show buds.

Taking a quick nibble, he continued, "Redneg, this is not just my opinion or some false belief. We have real proof of our real essence. You know that it is only because of the essence we have that we can exist as rabbits, and only as rabbits. That's not a restriction. That's a joy. It keeps us focused on being able to live fully instead of having to figure out how we should live. I would suggest that you and Rebil ask whether two rabbits could give birth to a fox and a squirrel."

Redneg stopped nibbling the tulips. "You and your kind just don't get it. But if you or your litter don't start respecting Squipples and Foreal, I'll be talking to the council."

Rater knew better than to say anything else. From what he had heard from other rabbits, the council worked on a principle that accusations were true until proven false. The rabbits from areas where the new thinking had taken hold were being forced to accept the lie that there was no real truth. And when accusations of intolerance or old thinking were brought forth, the rabbit in question was guilty until proven innocent.

The two rabbits parted ways, leaving some of the tulip buds untouched. The tension of the conversation robbed them both of an appetite for the human's spring flowers.

Rater shared with Rajina the events and conversations that had taken place. Rajina hung her head. She, like Rater, was heartbroken. They clearly could see the terrible path that Rial and Rompy were heading down. They were fearful that the beautiful and good existence that they, and generations before, had lived was somehow now at risk.

The next day Rompy bit Risky. Risky turned around and snapped at his neighbor and friend, "Now cut that out! You're not a hunter, you're a rabbit. I'm not your prey and you're not a predator, so stop the nonsense! And don't be going and running to your father to come and yell at me either."

But Rompy did exactly that and raced across the yard to where his father was eating some new grass.

Redneg came bounding full speed over to Risky.

"What is your problem? How can you be so insensitive and bigoted? I'll be taking you to the council!"

Risky decided that he could no longer obey his parents' advice to respect his elders, and instead needed to speak to what was true. He stood up and fluffed his fur to its fullest, facing the screaming Redneg.

Lowering his ears and pulling in his whiskers, he spoke deliberately to the older rabbit, "I don't really care what you do. Your son bit me and the next time he does that, he'll have bitten the wrong rabbit. I'm not being insensitive and I'm not being bigoted. I'm seeing facts. A rabbit bit me like he thought he could eat me. If it had really been a fox, I'd have run. But it wasn't a fox, it was a rabbit. And the next time that rabbit bites me, he will be sorry he did. I have the essence of a tough, mean and strong rabbit... and I will take great joy in living up to all my rabbitness."

Redneg was not expecting such a strong comeback. He had failed to notice that Risky had indeed developed the gifts that he had been born with and was now a rabbit that would be tough to contend with. Redneg summoned up enough of his own tattered toughness to blurt out a "we'll see about that!"

Risky turned his back on Redneg and casually nibbled on the greens in front of him.

P. F. Armstrong

17
Love Tested

"But what really bothers me is that I thought my best friend would support me."

Feeling a kindred encouragement by her brother's foxy claimed identity, Rial spent many hours figuring out how to be more squirrelly. Redneg was ever supportive, encouraging her more and more to live as a squirrel. Rebil had a sense of pride in the courage her daughter had and while she wondered how her squirrel daughter would become a rabbit mom, she was always outwardly supportive.

Romi enjoyed playing with her friend. She avoided as much as she could the squirrel issue, but it was becoming harder each day to see past it. While Romi nibbled on the grass, Rial tried to climb trees. Romi would help Rial up time and time again as her friend tumbled off the tree trunks, her rabbit feet having no way to hold on. Romi learned to just be quiet when Rial insisted that she'd be able to climb them soon enough.

Romi was always watching her words even though she considered Rial a dear friend. She would express her sympathy when Rial complained of stomach pains. Yet, Romi knew that rabbits were not meant to eat the nuts that Rial was continually trying to make the mainstay of her diet.

There were times though that Romi had to just walk away. Rial was attempting to physically change her body. She tried to attach branches to her back end to simulate a bushy squirrel tail. She would rub her ears against the trees, trying to make them small and squirrel like. Rial had convinced herself that those beautiful trademarks of a rabbit's profile were preventing her from being the tree leaping squirrel she claimed to be. She continually rubbed them raw on tree bark. Ear infections and headaches followed her continued efforts.

What bothered Romi the most was not that Rial was failing to recognize that she could not just be a squirrel based on her thoughts. Romi's deeper concern was that the time and efforts she spent being squirrelly were depriving her of growing into her essence as an adult rabbit. Rial was wearing out her teeth, ruining her hearing and damaging her strong back legs. The saddest part was that by using all of her time trying to be a squirrel, she was not learning how to use her rabbitness to survive, to become a healthy future mother of rabbits. Romi really believed that if and when Rial decided that being a squirrel was not really her essence, she would have already damaged her ability to then live fully as a rabbit.

It was an especially warm spring day. Romi was doing her best to help Rial as the young rabbit continued her attempts to climb the big pine tree. After the inevitable tumble out of the tree, Rial started to experience stomach pains.

Romi's concern for her friend became stronger than her tolerance to stay hushed.

"Rial, you know all those headaches and stomach pains you've been having?"

"Yes"

"Well, I'm pretty sure it because you're eating what the rodent squirrels eat, and we rabbits weren't made for that. And the headaches are probably because you're doing things to your ears that if I did that, I'd have headaches also. You know, soon enough we'll be ready to be mother rabbits ourselves. I'm afraid you may be too sick to do that."

Rial's ear's tilted back as she gave Romi a disapproving look.

"You know, Romi, my parents told me you might try that little speech on me. You're just like your parents. You're stuck in that old thinking. But what really bothers me is that I thought my best friend would support me. I think it's your rejection that's giving me the headaches and stomach pains. And I think I've had enough of it."

Stunned by Rial's harsh interpretation of what had been a genuine desire to help alleviate her pains, Romi wasn't sure what to say next.

Rial continued, "You know, I'm just going to leave. Don't even think of trying to join me."

Rial bounced off and found her father, sharing with him how not even Romi would support her.

Redneg was infuriated. He immediately hopped over and yelled at Romi, "You are not a friend at all. You know, it's your judgmental attitude, your desire to keep Rial trapped in something she's not that is causing the headaches and stomach pains. If you really care that much, then why don't you just get out of her life so she doesn't have to deal with your insensitive intolerance anymore!"

Romi cowered under the shower of Redneg's verbal barrage. When she lifted her head, he was already gone. But screaming at Romi was not enough, Redneg also felt that he needed to take his case to Romi's parents.

He promptly hopped over to see Rater and Rajina. Redneg started yelling at both of them, declaring that their continuation in treating Rial as a rabbit, and refusing to call her by her squirrel name, was causing her stress. This was evident by Rial's development of stomach issues.

Rater wondered whether to say anything at all. Redneg did not seem to be in a learning or listening mood. But Rater cared about Rial and her health, her ability to follow the calling of her rabbitness.

"Redneg," he began, in a careful measured tone, "We rabbits know that we cannot eat seeds and nuts. They will cause stomach distress and we don't really have the teeth for them. So that is a very logical reason why Rial is having stomach issues. I'm sure that whatever confusion she's dealing with is also causing stress, and that won't help. As for the headaches, we see the tumbles she takes everyday trying to climb that tree. I'd certainly get headaches doing that as well."

Redneg listened, but his tilted ears showed his unwillingness to accept Rater's thoughtful assumptions to the underlying causes.

"Listen to me, Rater," Redneg began, in a menacing tone, "You and Rajina are the real reason. You teach your kids that nonsense about Mother Nature and the Master Craftsman so that you can always have some sort of dominance over them."

He lifted his ears, and tried to feign a tone of one who was ready to be reasonable. The words of Fucho echoed in his mind.

"You know, Fucho was right. You carry this story about the Craftsman as some sort of weapon to scare your kids into believing you. You are on some sort of power trip! I gave my kids freedom from all that, and they can choose who and what they are. The council warned us about the weapons you'd use, and I have it in my mind to tell them about you and this whole incident."

Rater and Rajina's thoughts were identical. "What did he mean by 'incident'? It was just one bunny telling a friend what he thought to help stop stomach pains and headaches."

Rater and Rajina's concerns about the safety of their children grew. They wondered how such a good friendship could have come to this. How could they keep their fellow rabbits from danger if they ignored their own rabbitness? They mourned that their good friends seemed to be rebelling against what Mother Nature had designed.

The couple said nothing else, as they had been hearing tales from other creatures who had wandered through the garden. They reported stories of how those who had stayed strong with the wisdom of the ages were isolated and outcast, as if that wisdom was now the poison. Rater and Rajina did not want to find a new place to live. They were well aware of the dangers of their current dwelling, and to move would mean new dangers of which they were not aware. They did not want to put their next litter of bunnies into that life threatening situation.

Romi had followed Redneg but was staying at a distance. Redneg's discourse re-ignited the confusion that Gabbadon had sown. She thought of her own situation as a runt, wanting dearly to think of herself as a full-sized rabbit. She felt like a normal rabbit, ate like a normal rabbit, and had all the gifts of a normal rabbit except for size and speed. But no matter how much Romi identified herself as a normal rabbit, the truth was that the Master Craftsman had made her a runt. She believed her parents advice to respect that truth, and to ignore that obvious fact would probably lead to her being a convenient snack for a predator. Her near-death experience, at the talons of Hank the hawk, had proven that.

Romi retreated to her burrow, wondering how she'd ever be able to help her friend.

18
Reality Flies In

> *"... let her pride block the good intentioned warning..."*

Hank the hawk had nursed his damaged pride. He returned to the airways above the human gardens, scouting out whether the rabbits were absorbed in nibbling tender new flower shoots. He made slow circling motions very high in the sky, thankful that on this cloudy day his shadow was barely perceptible on the lawn. He hoped it would prevent his presence from being detected by the rabbits who had honed their rabbit senses.

Thanks to his hawk vision, given by the Craftsman, he was able to see the happenings at ground level despite being well aloft in the sky. He carefully observed the rabbits going about their business.

Today, he caught sight of something very peculiar. Something so peculiar that Hank wondered if Mother Nature was playing tricks on him. But he soon discarded that thought, as Mother always played by the rules.

There was a young rabbit trying to climb a tree.

Thoughts raced through the hawk's mind. "Could that rabbit have a vision problem? That's really rare for a rabbit. Could it really think it can climb a tree? No, that would mean the rabbit is defying the very essence that was given to it by the Craftsman. And besides, wouldn't that rabbit realize that the tree is no safer from me than the ground? Apparently it doesn't talk much about me with the squirrels."

Hank's mind wandered to the unsuspecting squirrel that had recently become his midday meal.

Hank studied this strange sight some more. He looked for a pattern, a set of movements he could predict would happen. That way he would be able to direct his descent perfectly.

The hawk's hunger allowed him to ignore that this was defying all that he knew about rabbits. Hank noticed that when the rabbit, who seemed to have something stuck to his tail, would jump towards a low branch, it would make an attempt to hang on. Inevitably, it could not, and would tumble to the ground. Rabbits apparently are not made to gracefully fall out of trees, he thought. But that tumble resulted in a few seconds of the rabbit regaining its steadiness on all fours.

Hank knew that rabbits had been given keen hearing, wide eyesight and strong powerful legs. When they combined those gifts from the Craftsman, with the nurturing of their rabbitness as Mother intended, it made any attempt to snatch one a delicate balance of surprise timing and calculated descent. But this rabbit gave him a special opportunity. In the world of predator and prey, a second or two was like a gift to the pursuer. Not only would this rabbit be clueless about Hank's descent, she'd also be slow in her first moves to escape.

Hank smiled to himself. He had a plan.

Hank continued to circle. He noticed another rabbit nearby. Its ears were not twitching. Even that rabbit had not been alerted to the aerial presence of its predator. That would mean a call out announcing his descent would be too late.

Hank saw the rabbit setting up to make another jump towards the tree. The tree had a low branch. He circled to ensure that he was perfectly aligned with the soft breeze, for a quick and silent descent.

Romi was completely engrossed in today's sprouts in the garden. She was only slightly paying attention to Rial's continued attempts to climb the tree.

As she rooted around, she noticed an ever so slight change in the gray cloudy light. Romi focused her rabbit instincts on what that could mean. She realized that the fast passing, nearly invisible shadow was from high above. Romi stopped nibbling. She raised her head. Her peripheral vision caught sight of wings, silhouetted against the sun shielding clouds.

Romi hollered, "Rial, I think the hawk is coming. We need to be ready to hide. Go towards the thicket at the fence."

Rial, who was completely focused on being a squirrel, yelled back. "You need to respect me! I'm a squirrel!" She poised herself at the tree, and then added, "And will you stop calling me the wrong name! I'm Squipples!"

Romi saw the shadow continuing to circle. She sent out the warning. The tall ears of the nearby herbivores quickly picked up the call. Their instincts understood. They all made sure that they were close or heading to shelter. All of them except Rial. She continued lining up to make a jump into the tree, convinced that with a good start, she'd be able to climb like a squirrel should.

Rebil was nearby. She had somewhat heard the conversation between the Romi and Rial. Despite her instincts telling her to heed the warning, the mother in her, influenced by the new thinking, heard something else. She had heard Rial's agitation at not being called Squipples.

Romi yelled again, "Rial, you have to get ready to run!"

Rial only heard her rabbit name and let her pride block the good intentioned warning that Romi had sent.

Squigs and Squags, who had been amused watching Rial's antics, got serious when they saw the alarmed rabbits. Their keen peripheral vision caught sight of the now descending hawk. They scampered around the tree trunk, using its girth as a barrier between them and the hawk. Their squirreliness equipped them to stay out of sight, as they found an inaccessible niche in which to hide.

Rial had already lost some of her rabbit instincts. In trying to get rid of her ears, they no longer were as acute in hearing as the ones bestowed on her at birth.

She made another run to the tree. Again, her rabbit feet refused to latch onto the bark. She tumbled off a branch and onto the ground.

Rebil now grasped the danger in what was happening. She made a run towards Rial, who was groggily getting back on her feet.

Hank was brimming with confidence. He had timed his descent perfectly. The peculiar rabbit had fallen out of the tree and was wobbling, as it made its way to its feet. Hank noticed another rabbit zig zagging to safety. But he also saw a rabbit continuing to warn his intended victim, and actually running into the very area that he was honed in on. Hank wondered momentarily if he should set his sights on that slightly plumper rabbit.

Hank's dim shadow now covered both rabbits. Rebil thought she had time, but she was still a few leaps away. She watched in painful sadness as two talons latched into Rial. The young rabbit squealed in panic and pain.

Romi heard the squeal and turned in time to see Rial being taken airborne. She felt a stabbing ache in her heart.

Rebil slumped to a standstill as her progeny disappeared. Her body shook and her ears went limp as grief, frustration and anguish overwhelmed her. She had not been able to save her daughter Rial.

P. F. Armstrong

19
Blame Game

"It's time you woke up and stopped
your preaching about following
Mother Nature."

Redneg saw all that had happened. He saw Rebil, now slumped in sadness. He knew that he lived in a predator-prey world and had seen scenes like this before.

Redneg hopped over to the mother of his litter. She lifted her head, as the sadness in her eyes turned to fury. Rebil believed she knew the real reason why Rial was gone.

"It's all Romi's fault! She kept calling her 'Rial' and that bothered Squipples so much that she got distracted from escaping. Something needs to be done to stop this!"

Redneg ignored all that he knew about the predator and prey drama. He believed that he now had someone to blame, convincing himself that it wasn't Mother Nature at all. It was those rabbits who were continuing to imprison his family with their old thinking.

He hopped angrily over to Romi's family burrow, bursting in on Rajina and Rater, who were still hiding from the hawk's invasion.

"You two and your hateful daughter caused my Squipples to be killed by the hawk! It's time you woke up and stopped your preaching about following Mother Nature. Your Romi distracted poor Squipples. If Romi had only respected Squipple's being a squirrel, she probably would have been able to save herself. This is all your fault!"

Rajina and Rater were stunned!

Thoughts they never thought they would need to think raced through their mind.

Was Redneg implying that treating a rabbit like a rabbit was wrong?

Would encouraging Rial to be a squirrel actually have enabled her to climb that tree?

Would that have made it so that she could digest nuts properly?

The two rabbits knew that in a predator-prey world, they were prey. It was a part of the circle of life. They were the only survivors of all their litter mates. That is why they worked so diligently in teaching their bunnies how to be the best rabbits they could be, so that their children would go on to have children of their own.

Rajina summoned the courage to speak up to the fuming Redneg, "You must know that we are also heartbroken for Rial. You know that we treated her as we treat our own. But we refused to pretend that Rial's rabbit essence had become squirrel essence just because she thought so."

Redneg looked like he was ready to speak, but Rater quickly added to what Rajina had said, "Redneg, you know that since the beginning of time, Mother Nature has made it so that all creatures would go forth and multiply if we acted in accord with both our mind and our body. We are not only mind or only body. When our minds say one thing and our bodies say another, we set ourselves up for disaster. If my mind says I'm faster than my body says, I will set myself up to be the hawk's next victim. Our body is a reality. Our mind is our belief. When beliefs don't recognize reality, we live in a state of confusion. And that is very contrary to the clarity that Mother Nature orchestrates."

Redneg was again ready to speak, but Rajina cut in, "We acted out of love, and sometimes that love needs to be tough. When Romi daydreams of not being a runt, our job is to make sure her daydreams don't block reality. True love pulls one out of danger, even when it's tough and even when the loved one can't see the danger themselves. When we directed Rial away from her squirrel beliefs, that was our intent. And that included not calling her Squipples. The new thinking would have us believe that we get to make all the rules. We see the great danger in that."

115

Rajina paused for just a short moment. "Redneg, it seems to me that you and Rebil substituted being a parent with being a friend to your litter. As a result, you mistook tolerance for true kindness. In doing so, you refused to guide them on the paths that we know from generations of rabbithood to be the best chance for our survival as prey in a predator filled world."

Rajina and Rater could see the fury in Redneg's eyes as his ears leaned back. He was still immensely hurting at the tragic loss of his young progeny. Yet, he clung to the idea that somehow this was the fault of those who failed to support Rial in her belief that she was a squirrel.

He was fed up with all this nonsense about respecting Mother Nature that Rajina and Rater kept spouting. He thought that if the Master Craftsman was a caring Master, then he wouldn't have to live in a predator-prey world, that creatures could be whatever they wanted to be and do whatever they wanted. To him, following Mother Nature was more like a devious scheme, making him a prisoner to a life he never chose. He certainly did not see the Mother's plan as the fantasy which Rajina and Rater allowed themselves to be duped into.

Redneg glared at the two rabbits that he no longer considered friends. His voice lowered into a stern tone, "If you two and your family don't start respecting what my young rabbits choose to be, then I will need to go and see what the council has to say."

Rajina and Rater were starting to think that Redneg just might make good on that threat. Despite that threat, they stayed strong, not ready to abandon the Craftsman's designs or the Mother's ways. To them, staying clear of the dangerous new thinking was the best path to give future generations.

Rater nodded at Redneg, showing that he had heard what Redneg threatened. "I suspect that you see something in that new thinking that appeals to you." He shuffled his paws as he continued. "Rajina and I just don't see how good can come out of that new thinking. It defies the success of rabbit generations, actually all animal generations, as far back as anyone knows. We really think that we can't pretend our essence is central to who we are. Our essence is all we can truly pass on. It's our birthright.

Rater arched his shoulders. "If we as parents don't recognize and nurture that birthright, we set our offspring up for a terribly confused existence.

Inching a bit closer to Redneg, Rater concluded. "If you want to make sure that your offspring have offspring, I think you should consider what we've said."

Redneg kept his ears back and shrugged, "I've had enough with you!"

He turned, and with a strong bound, was soon out of sight.

P. F. Armstrong

20
Guile Begets Vile

> *"… it's you against the world. But you're smarter than those other rabbits."*

Redneg heard that Nishy was in the area. He wondered if the new thinking newt might give him some advice. Gabbadon had been closely watching Redneg's moves. The gecko was determined to keep the new thinking father on his new thinking path.

Gabbadon scurried off to see Nishy. "That rabbit father is wanting to see you. Make sure you follow through. Share with him how important it is to serve one's own will."

Nishy respected the gecko's influence. The newt spread the word that indeed she was in the area.

Redneg met Nishy near the shady stone wall. It was a great place for a carnivorous, insect seeking newt.

Redneg began, "Thank you so much for meeting me. I need your advice. As you may have heard, we have been getting disrespected by the old thinking rabbits, to the point where it led to the demise of my one daughter."

Nishy put her little hand up. Redneg stopped speaking.

"I know that there are many who, out of their own helplessness, hang on to the ideas about Mother Nature and the Master Craftsman. But you and your family have seen the better way. You know that you do not have to be slaves to this mysterious magic they call Mother Nature or the Craftsman. You have done well. Two of your children have taken the step to be their own master. By sheer will, all of your offspring can be whatever they want to be. Stay strong."

Redneg's look showed that he wanted to agree, but doubts started to creep into his mind.

Nishy saw that look. She took a deeper tone, "Look Redneg, it's you against the world. But you're smarter than those other rabbits. By embracing the better thinking, you've made yourself sort of a super rabbit, the master of a new race of rabbits."

The words had their intended effect. Redneg soaked them in, their intoxicating promise feeding his ego. He knew what he needed to do next. He thanked the newt who, having seen that her advice had taken hold, was already in pursuit of a nearby fly.

Redneg was full of sorrow, anger and self-righteousness. He now saw himself as the one who would make sure that his family would not be slaves of that old thinking, the Mother Nature, Master Craftsman garbage that filled the other rabbits' minds.

He called his family together.

"I know that we are all hurting from the loss of Squipples. Some of you may be hearing from your friends that this was all just part of Mother Nature's way. It wasn't. Squipples was not being respected for her decision to be a squirrel and those same friends that talk about Mother Nature are the ones most to blame. They caused poor Squipples to be stressed out and that caused other problems. And on the very day that she was snatched by the hawk, she was being bothered by Romi. And that's why she didn't survive!"

Rompy listened carefully. He spoke up, "Do you think if Squipples had gone to the squirrels that they would have accepted her as one of their own?"

Redneg paused for a few moments. "Great question, Foreal."

The litter's father had emphasized "Foreal", sending a message to his other children who were still struggling to understand their brother's decision to be a fox.

The patriarch continued, "That would only have worked if those squirrels had been smart enough to adopt the new thinking. And, from my observation, they have not."

Rompy thought this over. He realized what he now needed to do.

Redneg saw his son thinking this over. "Well, Foreal, the good news is that you've identified yourself as a predator. That will keep you safer than Squipples."

Rebil chimed in, "You know, Foreal, that we want you to be happy in who you think you are. We'll support you in whatever you choose."

Rebil's complete focus on giving Rompy his freedom prevented her from seeing the danger in the ill-advised promise she had just made.

Rompy swelled with pride each time his parents called him Foreal. He noticed that several of his siblings were listening closely, but seemed to still struggle with what their parents were saying.

He thought back on what Gabbadon had said. The words of his parents, along with the gecko's advice, made him believe all the more that he was truly a fox. He let the desire to be his own master chip away at the obvious evidence that he was prey.

Rompy ran off from the family meeting. He realized what he needed to immediately do.

Gabbadon saw the young rabbit leaving. He cackled with delight. He was sure he knew what was on Rompy's mind.

21

False Friendship

"Quite frankly, you have too much courage to be a rabbit."

Gabbadon made a quick visit to Forster the fox. His cunning disguise kept him hidden while he gave the sly predator his contrarian advice. "Don't eat the next visitor who wanders into your company."

Forster was biding his time, wondering what the gecko's strange advice was all about. He sniffed along the edge of the garden property.

Rompy knew the spot well. He had been warned to steer clear of there by all the elder bunnies. But Rompy was confident that his identity as a fox would make it different for him.

Forster was a typical fox. He was cunning enough so that he could be lazy. He made his rounds to the nearby coops that had the likes of chickens, guineas and ducks, hoping to find one left open. He made his rounds past the areas where he knew the rabbits were hiding, hoping that one may have been a bit late in returning to safety.

As he laid in the grass, he saw what he thought must be a dream. A lone rabbit resolutely heading in his direction. He was ready to move from his relaxed pose to his ready to pounce position when the words of Gabbadon echoed in his mind.

"Well, well," he thought to himself, "that wily little amphibian gave me some curious advice. I guess I'll just keep myself right here. Nothing to fear from even a courageous little rabbit."

Rompy came within speaking distance, his rabbitness still trying hard to keep him from danger.

Rompy spoke up, "Good evening, I believe you are the one called Forster."

Forster's ego swelled a bit. Apparently, he was well known in the rabbit circles.

"That is quite true," he replied, "And to whom may I be speaking?"

"My name is Foreal," replied the rabbit.

Forster shook his head. He puzzled over the introduction in his mind. "Foreal is clearly not a rabbit name. Actually, it's a fox name. Why in the world would a rabbit come here... that's puzzling all by itself, but now introducing itself with a fox name?"

Forster slowly realized why the gecko had paid him a visit.

"Well, Foreal, it's a pleasure to meet you. Can I be of some help?" Forster almost laughed at hearing his own implausible sentence leave his mouth.

Rompy was still a bit anxious, being within leaping distance of this large-toothed carnivore. But the words of his father, to be his own master, steeled his nerves.

"My name is Foreal because I am not a rabbit. I'm a fox."

Forster was a bit stunned. He realized how brilliant the gecko's advice really was.

The real fox composed himself. "That's quite remarkable, and I must say that I can see why. You have the courage of a fox to be sure. Quite frankly, you have too much courage to be a rabbit."

The fox's words fed Rompy's desire to be his own master. "Yes," he thought, "I am too courageous to be a rabbit. I am indeed a fox."

Forster's lazy cunning instincts took over. Why would he need to chase a rabbit ever again? His clever mind hatched an idea, rolling the thoughts over in his mind.

"What if I were to identify myself as a rabbit?" he thought, "Why, they'd have to accept me into their burrow, wouldn't they? Now, how wonderfully delicious would that be?"

He replied to the little rabbit, "Well, Foreal, it is quite my pleasure to have you here. We will surely become good friends. So, please tell me about yourself."

Rompy relaxed with the welcoming words of the fox. He was soon sharing with Forster where all the burrows were, how many siblings he had, where their favorite eating places were and even shared the sad story about Rial.

He was just concluding that story, "So, you see, it's those backward thinking, former friends of ours that caused her to be killed. My father is a very smart rabbit. He's going to help our entire community be more free, once the rest of them adopt the new thinking."

Forster had heard of the new thinking. He himself did not really care one way or another. He had no problem with what the Craftsman had given him, and he found ways to get along with the rules of Mother Nature. But, in the spirit of forging this friendship, he nodded approvingly at what the rabbit was saying.

Rompy concluded, "Forster, I must be going back now, but I wanted to make sure that you knew that I am now a fox. I really appreciate your friendship and respect of my decision."

Forster feigned the best genuine smile he could, suppressing the giddy excitement that was building inside of him.

22

Dangerous Deception

"You are stuck in your binary
thinking that there are just predator
and prey."

Forster strode up to the edge of the area where the rabbits were grazing. He put his weight on both back legs, making as small a jump as he could, and attempted to land on both front feet. This was not his normal mode of moving, but he was trying to be rabbit like.

The rabbits saw the awkwardly moving fox, but it was still a fox. They all ran for their hiding places. Rebil and Redneg made sure that their young rabbits had all made it to their assigned burrow holes before squeezing into their own.

Forster saw Rompy was still out. "Ah, Foreal, it's so good to see you." The fox tried his best to be as innocent sounding as possible.

Rompy replied, his nervousness betrayed by a slight quiver of his fur, "Well, Forster, I didn't expect you to visit us."

His pride subdued his rabbit instincts to escape, but part of his brain still rebelled, as the words came out, "But, of course, you're welcome."

Rispy was hiding in a burrow nearby. She couldn't believe what she was hearing. How could her brother think it was safe to bring a fox into their home?

Forster tried to stay calm, but his foxy essence was naturally excited with the scent of bunny meat all around him. He fought back the urge to pounce. Instead, he continued his calm conversation.

"You know, Foreal, you made me realize something about myself that has been bothering me for some time now. You see, I really like carrots and I have an inclination to hop everywhere. I really think that I am a rabbit."

Rompy wasn't sure what to say. He backed up to the burrow in which his parents were hiding.

Forster made his best attempts at looking like he was hopping towards the barely noticeable hole near the fence post.

"Hey, in there!" he called, his voice sounding as if he was delivering some good news. "I'm not really a fox. I'm a rabbit trapped in a fox body. The other foxes make fun of me and pick on me. They don't respect me. They all think that I'm confused. Will you guys accept me? I like carrots, spinach and other veggies." Forster made a calculated pause. "Can I come in?"

Rebil realized that silence was of no use. The fox knew they were in there. She muttered a response, "Why, our burrow is not sized for you.   You'll need to go somewhere else. So sorry!"

At that point Forster knew what to do next. He pulled his head back, pretending to appear indignant. Then, in a voice that bordered between hurt and anger, he proclaimed, "You're just like those old thinking foxes. You make your holes so that only traditional rabbits can use them. You are stuck in your binary thinking that there are just predator and prey. How about me? I'm neither predator nor prey... I have a good mind to talk to the council!"

Redneg stuttered a reply, "Don't do that, Forster. We can make it right. Just see. Come back tomorrow."

Forster kept his act going, "Ok, I'll see what tomorrow brings. I hope that you realize that you should be accepting all who identify as rabbits. I really thought that you would not be so old fashioned in your thinking."

P. F. Armstrong

23
Mother Is Real

*"The telltale signs of Mother Nature
were on the lawn…"*

Rajina and Rater watched in puzzlement, as their neighbor rabbits worked tirelessly, making their burrow bigger.

"How weird?" they thought, knowing that Forster now knew where they all lived.

Rater could not resist. He wandered over to his former friend.

"Redneg, what are you doing? Rabbits don't live in burrows with big holes… that could let anyone in. Why just yesterday you had a fox here!"

Redneg was working hard, kicking dirt, and didn't feel like replying. He knew that Rater would be too stuck in his old-fashioned thinking to understand.

Forster spent the morning talking to his fox friends, outlining where the burrows were. They were all applauding Forster for his extremely cunning plan. The evening would be a delight.

Redneg told all his children that they needed to make their burrows more inclusive, able to accept rabbits who did not come in traditional rabbit sizes. Rompy happily followed his father's advice. All of the others made half-hearted attempts, as they had enough rabbitness to be nervous about making a fox-friendly entrance to their safe burrow. Rispy thought this was crazy. She realized that her burrow was no longer safe, and moved to another location with the help of Romi.

Rebil and Redneg were exhausted. All the digging had left them tired, and they had not spent as much time grazing. Despite the gaping hole that let in the cool night air, they fell asleep quickly.

Rajina and Rater told their young rabbits to find other places to hide. It seemed that the fox knew too much. Helping them find other places left no time for them to find one for themselves. They made sure to deepen their burrow. They squeezed into the furthest corner.

Forster and three of his friends slinked into the area. No longer was Forster pretending to move like a rabbit. His foxiness was all business tonight.

Rajina and Rater heard the light footsteps of the encroaching canines. They stayed huddled deep in their burrow, breathing as little as possible.

A shadow covered the entrance. They knew that a fox was there. Summoning up all of their rabbitness, they transformed themselves into a stone like stillness.

The shadow passed over.

Soon, they heard the horrible sounds of rabbits in distress. They heard the cackling joy of foxes locking onto their prey. For what seemed an eternity, they heard the screams of their neighbors and friends. In reality, it was only moments long. Rompy's conversation with Forster had made the foxes' attack an easy one.

The next morning, Rajina and Rater looked out from their burrow. Their stomachs churned as their eyes took in the gory landscape. The telltale signs of Mother Nature were on the lawn: prey fur and predator prints.

Lurking in the thicket nearby was Gabbadon, smiling that his plot had succeeded. Soon there would be rabbit parts attracting flies and creating maggots. He would not have to work hard for a few meals. Gabbadon smiled. He indeed would be the lord of the flies.

24
The Good Beauty of Truth

> *"Our job as parents was to help you be rabbits, to be who you are and be that well."*

Romi went over to where Rispy was hiding. Romi knew that Rispy would know what had happened. Romi stopped at the small entrance. She saw Rispy in a tight ball, her body shaking with sobbing. Romi moved quietly beside her, saying nothing.

Rispy looked up. Her eyes were swollen. "I don't get it," she stuttered. "How could my parents and siblings not see this coming?"

The orphaned rabbit looked down. "Should I have stayed with them? Was I wrong to leave?"

Romi stayed quiet, letting Rispy wrestle through her thoughts.

The two sat in silence for a while. Rispy looked at the friend who saved her life. "Thank you. You really are a true friend."

Rispy turned and faced the burrow entrance. "Now what do I do?"

Romi nodded her head towards the yard. "You come with me. We'll figure this out."

The two headed towards where Romi's family was huddling together.

Rajina and Rater, heartbroken at the tragic loss of their friends saw Romi and Rispy coming towards them.

Rajina hopped over towards Rispy, as she whispered, "You know that you can always consider us as your family."

The air still had the stink of death. This was unlike anything they had ever seen, so unlike those times when it was a predator-prey orchestration of Mother Nature. This was the result of decisions made in defiance of her sensible order and lack of trust in the essence given them by the Master Craftsman.

They looked at their offspring, now ready to be fully capable rabbits. Rater started talking to them, softly and sadly, "It doesn't matter whether or not you have every rabbit trait, such as liking carrots or spinach. Truth be told, I'm not a big fan of kale." Risky chuckled a little.

Rater maintained a respective tone. "We must accept that we are both mind _and_ body. We are not mind _or_ body."

The young rabbits nodded as their father continued. "In other words, we can use our thoughts to guide what we actually have in amazing ways. But we can't rely on thoughts alone and ignore the reality."

Rowdy spoke up. "But I don't get it." He looked over at Rispy, as he continued. "Those parents seemed so cool. There were several times I kind of wished I was Rispy's brother."

Rater acknowledged Rowdy's comment. "I know that sometimes you think your mother and I were too tough. That we did not allow you to pursue your imaginations."

He wiggled his head, showing off his beautiful ears, as he continued. "We were created to be rabbits. Our job as parents was to help you be rabbits, to be who you are and be that well. We know that there will always be times of doubt, despair and confusion but our job is to keep you grounded... to keep mind and body united, not divided. When Risky acted as if he were a lone wolf, we appreciated his courage but we made sure that he was always honest with the reality that he was still a rabbit... that going out into the yard was always a danger. When Rowdy and Ruffy thought they were tougher than most rabbits, in size and speed, we made sure to keep them in line and respect the reality that they were still only rabbit fast. As you have learned, our world has predators who can outrun even the fastest rabbit."

Rajina chimed in, "Yes, while I may let my ego tell me I'm the fastest rabbit on earth, I must always respect the obvious fact of how fast I actually am. That I am, in fact, not the fastest rabbit on earth." The mother lifted her hind leg as she said "not", making sure her point was clear.

"While I can pretend all I want, I need to respect the facts. If I don't, I'll just be the next predator's meal."

Rater continued, "I know that you thought that maybe we were not being nice when we refused to accept the claim of Rial being a squirrel or Rompy being a fox. Truth be told, we were just being rabbit adults who desired to equip young rabbits with the ability to become adult rabbits themselves. Yes, we may all experience times of confusion about our rabbitness and we need to work through that. But we must never lose sight that Mother Nature is a fact. We were given rabbit bodies and rabbit instincts to be great rabbits. We get to decide how we accept or reject these realities, but that does not change the reality."

At this point, he looked at Rispy. "Your parents were wonderful rabbits. But I fear that they were fooled by some very cruel new thinking. In your gut, you knew how to stick to your rabbitness. That was courageous. And I know that you will always miss your siblings and parents. You know that you are welcome to be part of ours."

Rater looked skyward as he continued. "As we go through our days, our minds sometimes portray other potentials, some of those achievable and some not. But we must never lose sight of our biological realities, our essence. We must realize that there are truths in this life that Mother Nature will enforce. We are not the Master Craftsman. We are not our own craftsman. We are the creatures, not the Creator."

Rajina added, "No matter what, continue to be good rabbits, looking out for all other rabbits. While we believe that our best chance at survival is to use the rabbitness we were endowed with, we must share that belief with care and candor. Because while being confused and ridiculed is not something we would wish on anyone, we also do not want to invite the fate that befell our dear neighbor friends. Sometimes real love means pointing out the real facts."

P. F. Armstrong

Epilogue

News of the rabbit tragedy spread quickly through the woods. The Council reflected on where their new thinking had led the rabbits. Nishy held onto her beliefs. She found it easy to blame it all on the rabbits. That was a convenient way for her to rationalize it. After all, she thought that rabbits were just not intended to be a super species anyway.

Fucho did not even see it as a tragedy, but rather an affirmation of his belief life was futile.

Rater was glad to hear of the council's weakened influence on his fellow creatures. He wondered what had happened to Sarty. Animals traveling through told assorted tales that Sarty had realized how wrong his thinking had been. They told how Sarty had taken thoughtful notice of how the foxes took the new thinking to its logical conclusion. That had caused him to question his view on the new thinking. In particular, he began to doubt his claim that there was no Master Craftsman. He began to see that there must be an ultimate source of truth, and only an ultimate source. His followers were upset when he spoke about this. He quietly slipped out of popular view.

Some even told stories that the salamander, who had blatantly preached the non-existence of the Craftsman, recanted in his last days. And that in reconnecting with the Master, he felt a joy that he had never experienced before, a warmth in his cold-blooded veins.

Romi still missed playing with her friend. She and Rispy became close friends. Rispy accepted Rajina's offer and soon counted herself as part of Romi's family.

The two were chomping down on the now fully grown late spring vegetation. They heard the humans tossing stuff at the compost pile. Peering over, Romi's keen eyes saw what was there. She gave the signal, and, as always, her bigger siblings and even Rispy were fast outrunning her. But she accepted this reality as a runt. She, with her keen rabbit senses, had provided a value in alerting them to the new treasure. That was who she was, and she lived that well.

As she approached the pile, she noticed a new rabbit racing in. This was an especially rabbity rabbit.

Romi smiled to herself.

She sent a signal, a very female rabbit signal. The visiting rabbit turned and moved towards Romi. She playfully darted away and then back towards the compost pile. The new rabbit followed, doing a few leaps in the air along the way.

They arrived together. Rispy saw them arrive and gave Romi a little smirk.
There on top of the pile was the fresh feast that the humans had tossed out. Romi looked at the new rabbit. He introduced himself as Rex and nudged a special treat in her direction.

Romi looked at what he had slid in front of her. She smiled to herself and nodded gratitude to her new friend. Her rabbit instincts told her that he would be the right rabbit for her. Romi sensed that he would be strong in continuing to live the truth, the beauty and the good design of the Master Craftsman. That he would respect the guidance of Mother Nature.

What she saw in her mind was a fulfillment of her purpose, to give good life to the next generation. That seemed pretty amazing, even though she was a runty rabbit.

Now it was time to enjoy her new friend's gift. What could be better than a collection of candy like carrots?

About the Author

PF Armstrong's career has evolved from engineering to leadership team building to organic farming. What PF learned along the way is that if you break the laws of physics, people get hurt; if you break the laws of society, future generations get hurt; if you break the laws of mother nature, the continuation of life gets hurt.

Learning to live more organically has provided a fresh appreciation for the amazing design that the Master Craftsman put in place on the planet. PF, himself, learned to stop thinking that he was in a fight against Mother Nature. Learning to listen to and respect what she was teaching has led to nutritious discoveries. PF is humbled by the delicate and precious order put in place, a planetary biome that reflects the source of its Craftsman in truth, beauty and good.

For over a decade, his grandchildren have been challenging PF's knack for storytelling. Their wide-eyed requests for whimsical characters and ironic situations helped to birth this story.

The creatures in this tale are based on the critters that have decided to live in PF's garden. Though their chosen residence, amidst his vegetables, is not PF's preference, he has a certain admiration of the rabbits. Despite being a favorite meal of the nearby foxes, weasels and raptors, they seem to thrive. PF wondered what would happen if...

Made in the USA
Middletown, DE
17 March 2023

26998103R00086